CODE BLUE

CODE BLUE

*(Taking a fresh look at a set of laws
that may govern all things)*

SKIMORA

G.S.K. Mohan Rao

PARTRIDGE
A Penguin Random House Company

To order additional copies of this book, contact
Partridge India
000 800 10062 62
www.partridgepublishing.com/india
orders.india@partridgepublishing.com

CHAPTER 1

Place-London

"Ashley, listen, we've got to get cracking. You better search the house first. Let's hope we find some clue there," Chief Constable David Dickson of Scotland Yard spoke to his deputy Morgan Ashley

"O.K. David, I'll do that. By the way inspector Cooper phoned saying the luxury yacht Solaris was on its passage to the Isle of Wight, likely reaching there in a day or two."

Morgan rushed off in his squad car to 13, Queens Way, Kensington Gardens, owned by a Mr. Hazrara. A policeman was at the gate keeping vigil. Morgan started rummaging the house for possible clues or documents the Hazraras may have left behind. The family apparently was bundled out from their six—bedroom mansion. The furniture thrown helter—skelter was a sore sight in the Lobby, in the hall, in the bedrooms and elsewhere.

Inspector Cooper dropped in at the Hazrara house.

"Hello Ash, how is it going?"

"It's going but not too well. There are a lot of loose ends"

"I may be able to help. I went around finding out a few things about the family"

"Oh, O.K. Just put me in the picture. Who is Hazrara and what are the facts we know about him and his family?"

"The Hazraras were originally from India but were living in Africa. They had business interests in Uganda and Kenya. They left Uganda and settled down in London and expanded their business."

"What were they dealing in?"

"Nitin K. Hazrara owned a chain of retail outlets for children's clothes, toys and diamond jewelry. He also owned a network of budget hotels here in the United Kingdom and in Kenya. Hazrara in his early fifties is married with two teenage children, a boy and a girl. He had bought this house some three years before. His wife is said to be a famous classical dancer"

"Fine, what next, I see that he has furnished his mansion with the latest style of consumer durables and artifacts. The furniture, the plumbing, the kitchen ensemble and wall fittings are in good taste as almost everything else in the house. This indeed is a modern home with the best available creature comfort one could wish for".

"Hazrara's yacht 'La Solaris; had earlier belonged to Senor Cardoz, a Spanish—American businessman if that is of any relevance." added Cooper by way of additional information. He hung around for a while and then left to continue his investigation.

Morgan diligently went about his business. His brief was to go through the house with a fine tooth-comb to get some solid clues to crack the case of the 'disappearance without a trace' of the entire Hazrara family two weeks ago. This fact surprisingly hadn't come to light till the General Manager of Hazrara's budget hotel—chain a Mr. Simpson contacted the police the previous evening and reported the matter.

"I was expecting instructions from Mr. Hazrara two weeks ago and again yesterday but all my attempts to contact Mr. Hazrara failed. My calls were never answered. I considered this strange and tried to see if Mr. Hazrara had gone on board his yacht" Simpson had said to the police chief

'What did you do then?"

"I called up the yacht's skipper on wireless asking him if the Hazraras were on board. The answer was negative. I then checked with the caretaker of the farmhouse in the Isle of Wight"

"What happened there?"

Jack told me that no one was staying there. I panicked and have now come to lodge a complaint with you".

The police then swung into action. They roped in a Mr. Brunswick stationed in London as the resident director of Mr. Hazrara's companies to assist them in the search. Mr. Brunswick said the Hazraras were planning to go on a holiday to the Isle of Wight. Their Yacht was scheduled to arrive shortly from Malta after a complete re-fit including dry-docking and painting of its hull and accommodation.

"I will involve the Foreign police if need be. An investigating team is already on its way to Southampton and to the Hook Von Holland in the Netherlands where ferries from London and Liverpool regularly ply carrying passengers" David had told Brunswick before sending Ashley across.

Ashley Morgan felt the case might involve people of other countries perhaps the French for a start. Morgan shot several photographs of the Hazrara mansion and its rooms. He also collected photographs of the family and their custom-built car from an album lying in the living room. Enquiries at various places including the High School of the Hazrara kids, the beauty parlour frequented by Hazrara's wife Tavleen and the 'Directors club' at 64, Thread-needle Street where Nitin Hazrara was a long standing member, revealed no further information.

The scenario assessed by the British police by that evening was as follows:

On Friday the 13th of June, Nitin Hazrara and his family were to take the afternoon flight to the Isle of Wight. He had earlier failed to charter a six-seater private plane from 'Hamilton Travels & Tours' a travel facilitator company that usually catered to customers' special requirements of small planes. The travel company was embarrassed for not providing Hazrara a family plane and was more than happy to book first class tickets for him and his family on 'Pronto Air' that had daily flights to the Isle of Wight. It was not clear as to when or how the Hazrara family left home on their way to the airport for catching a flight scheduled for departure at five p.m. The airlines listed them under 'No Show' for that flight. The Hazraras house in a state of disarray pointed to the possibility of outsiders forcibly entering and taking the family out despite a struggle. The Hazrara family not showing up for the flight, their expensive custom built car un-sighted, made the police suspect a kidnap operation ending most likely in the family being held captive in some secret location perhaps outside London or may be outside the British Isles. A red alert was sent out to all concerned to check exit points at airports; Seaports and border check posts for the missing car and for members of the Hazrara family. Brief details were flashed across. Also on the off chance that they may have boarded a ferry taking their car along, a search was made of all passenger records of the Southampton-East Cowes ferries, the channel—crossing ferries between London and the Hook von Holland and also the Holland—West German check posts for the past two weeks to see if there was a record of the Hazraras or their car passing through them. The police were puzzled to find the car missing. Logically it had to be either at the mansion at London or at the Isle of Wight. The question was, if the Hazraras were flying to the Isle of Wight, why was the car missing both at London and at the Isle of Wight?

Things were getting complicated and the police seemed perplexed.

"Mr. Hazrara and the family never turned up here at the farm house on Friday or on Saturday and I reported it to Mr. Brunswick after Mr. Simpson's phone call to me. Aye, I did. Mr. Brunswick said that perhaps they flew to Malta to board the yacht. I'm still waiting for them" said Jack Simmons the janitor of the Hazrara farm house in the Isle of Wight. Jack said that the farmhouse was kept ready at all times but rarely used. "Sometimes some of Mr. Hazrara's friends including the locals, Europeans and Kenyans used the farm house for a week or less at a time," said he.

"Why didn't you raise an alarm when the Hazraras didn't turn up at their farm house Mr. Brunswick?" asked Dickson meeting Brunswick the resident director of Mr. Hazrara's company in London later in the day.

"Well as a matter of fact, I don't interact with Mr. Hazrara on a daily or weekly basis. I report to him once every month giving details of turn—over from the hotel-chain and the retail outlets and give a written resume of significant events or other points of importance during the month covered in the report. He usually telephones me if he wants me at any particular time. Otherwise we only meet once a month. I never felt something was amiss since Mr. Hazrara had a host of people to arrange things including his travel as and when needed" said Brunswick adding "Now that we do know of the family's unexplained disappearance, I'm worried to death praying that they should be safe and well and nothing untoward should have happened to them. I am prepared to spend a million pounds if need be to get to the bottom of this mystery. So please spare no effort or expense whatsoever and get the Hazraras back home safely at the earliest. If a ransom is to be paid to a gang of kidnappers or anyone else I will be glad to arrange the cash upfront before you finally nab them if you feel confident enough that they would not harm him or his family because of your intervention" The police investigated the background and family details of Hazrara's chauffer Ronnie Dexter. Dexter was around 45, single and living in the basement quarters of the Kensington mansion of the Hazraras. Neighbors said Ronnie had been with the Hazraras serving them as Chauffer for the past ten years, much before the family moved to Kensington Gardens and was a loyal employee. They said he was a very decent peace-loving person and had no trouble with anyone in the neighborhood at Kensington Gardens. Enquiries were made if anyone had seen the car driven by Dexter leave the house. Luckily there was positive response from a person that saw the car with only Dexter in it leaving the mansion at around six in the morning on the fateful Friday the 13th of June. Morgan immediately set the ball rolling asking all check posts on the London-Southampton route for information on the car on the 13th morning, including gas stations en-route.

All efforts by the British police to trace the Hazrara family proved futile even after a week of concerted action. There was no clue of the route they may have taken. There was also no trace of the car or its driver. The Yacht owned by them arrived at the Isle of Wight and a thorough search revealed nothing of any consequence. The hope that some vital information would emerge from the skipper and the crew of the Yacht throwing some light on the case turned into despair, as they were equally surprised and shocked to know from the police of the Hazrara disappearance. The police could see that all those serving the Hazraras were extremely fond of the family and were sorry to see them disappear. Though reluctant to conclude one way or the other the police had to admit that the only possibility was that a gang had kidnapped the family and is hiding them somewhere. Their immediate hope was that someone from the kidnap gang would contact one of Hazrara's corporate offices or houses for ransom. Meanwhile the police would continue to explore all avenues to solve the mystery.

CHAPTER 2

London

Ronnie Dexter was a man of principles. A Welshman of the old school, he detested indiscipline and back talk particularly with those above one's social status. He was born in a village in Wales and had a typical Welsh sing-song way of English speech that differed from those from England, Scotland or Ireland. Ronnie passed high school O-levels and discontinued further education for lack of financial support from his family. However he was keen on studying Welsh history and culture as and when time permitted. He was thrilled at the welsh tradition of giving unique importance to Bards or poets of brilliance so ceremonially feted, wined and dined during the annual Eisteddfod festival.

He learnt to drive and took up employment of driving cars and trucks starting at the minimum wage level and quickly gaining experience and expertise to become a regular chauffer with a car renting agency based in London. Nitin Hazrara had been a regular customer of the agency and Dexter became his favorite. Dexter was comfortable with the way Hazrara treated him while on duty and was happy to become his regular employee when Nitin suggested it. The car renting agency helped Dexter make the change paying him his bonus before its due date considering the relationship the agency had with the Hazrara group.

On that early morning of Friday the 13th Dexter was driving the Hazrara Bentley to ferry point in Southampton to catch a ferry to East Cowes on the Isle of Wight.

He was looking forward to driving to the Hazrara farm house beyond the picturesque chain bridge on the river past the historic Osborne house where Queen Victoria had stayed with Prince Albert. Dexter loved the

Isle of Wight the great tourist spot on the river Medina with the bridge connecting both the Cowes the east and the West.

He slowed and stopped the vehicle gently when he saw a Policeman at the Rodham—underpass signaling him to stop. The next few minutes saw things happen so fast that Dexter had no clue. The policeman had got into the car and the car was driven into a ramp that opened up into a container on a truck. The next thing was that the truck was speeding away with the car lying in a closed container on it. It was doubtful if anyone noticed this operation.

As soon as uploading of the car into the container was accomplished, the policeman revealed his true identity to Albert Dexter.

"I am an officer of 'Ever-win Operators Ltd'. Believe you me; I'm sure as things stand no harm should come to you. I am to hand over the car to our clients and naturally you are included in the package. You have to be with us for a few hours more"

"You are thieves and thugs and will get punished for this criminal act. I feel sorry for you and those rascals that employed you to do this."

"Fine. I do understand your outrage but things are not going to change. Perhaps they may even decide to kill you or maim you'

"They'll suffer the consequences of their misdeeds. I care a hang if I live or die after this ignominy"

The truck traveled at speed and reached Newcastle on the river Tyne. The car was brought out from the container at a private yard. A tough looking fellow called Mike Trench along with his crew of three took over the car plus the driver Dexter who was handcuffed for 'his own safety'.

"Mr. Dexter, you are under my custody till I get word to release you. It'll not be too soon I'm afraid, as there is plenty to do meanwhile".

Mike Trench worked for Miller Smith (U.K) Ltd. No one had any idea or knew what activity the company was engaged in.

CHAPTER 3

Minas, Uruguay

This small town Minas near Montevideo in Uruguay with its criss—crossing streets was like any other small town in Latin America. Most of its people at normal hours could be seen moving about in smart fashionably designed dresses with hardly anyone in tattered or worn out clothing signifying a moderately high standard of living. However one could sense in them a feeling of fear and dread that was palpable and scary. Men and women that passed on the streets in this tiny town hurried along without stopping. They never looked anyone in the eye. Perhaps they deliberately wished to avoid conversation especially with those they didn't know or recognize. It was utterly strange and positively unnerving. The reason was the recent cycle of events involving a haphazard pattern of sudden disappearance of men and women without a trace. It was inexplicable.

Nitin Hazrara was perplexed. He had come to this place accompanied by an escort purportedly for holding discussions prior to closing a big commercial deal worth more than two billion dollars. Things seemed to be happening to him very fast. It had all started in London. As he was preparing to leave his home in Kensington Gardens with his wife and kids, there was this phone call.

"I am Riaz Salim, speaking from the Embassy of Suleimania. I am the personal secretary to His Excellency the Ambassador of Suleimania in London, May I speak to Mr. Hazrara please?"

"This is Hazrara here. Please go ahead."

"I am contacting you Mr. Hazrara under the instructions of the president of Suleimania. We have an important message to be delivered to you. Some one from our Embassy is already on his way to meet you to discuss a very huge financial deal which could benefit you immensely."

"I am grateful, but would request you to kindly excuse me. I am not interested in making any deals just now. I am proceeding out of here on holiday and will be back after a fortnight. I could perhaps contact you then"

"Please Sir, Just listen. Please wait for our man who is already on his way to your house with a letter from the Ambassador. Just spare a few minutes please"

Hazrara thought it was wise to wait for this man from the embassy as it would be impolite to do otherwise. His flight to the Isle of Wight wasn't taking off till five in the evening and it was only noon. Hazrara's car had already been dispatched to the Isle of Wight to receive the family on arrival there. A rented car was scheduled to arrive at the house to pick them up at three thirty. Thus there was enough time he felt.

"Alright I will meet your man. What is his name?"

"Thank you Mr. Hazrara. Our Mr. Hauptman will meet with you."

Hauptman came after a little while. He was a German national.

"It is my pleasure to meet with you Mr. Hazrara. I work for the president of Suleimania. I am to give you this letter from the Ambassador."

Hazrara read the letter and understood the purpose.

"I have an extra vehicle accompanying the embassy car. Proper arrangements have already been made for you and the family to travel in great comfort to Huntington from where the next program would be made known." Hauptman said adding "At the end of it all there will be this big deal that will have to be signed by you personally in a Latin American country. While I cannot give you the name of the Latin American country, I can reveal that the deal would involve more than two billion dollars worth of contracts for various things including the setting up of a chain of budget hotels".Hazrara questioned him closely" The whole thing is so confidential that I dare not reveal the modus operandi. We want you to confirm your interest." Hauptman said. Hazrara thought over the matter and after consulting his wife Tavleen finally agreed. However Hazrara had insisted on talking to the ambassador of Suleimania and a formal call was put through by Hauptman and the Ambassador had authenticated the two billion dollar contract possibility to Hazrara's satisfaction.

"Mr. Hazrara, please do not contact anyone lest the information leaks out alerting our competitors." Hauptman warned.

Nitin Hazrara, Tavleen and the kids were requested by Hauptman to maintain utmost secrecy and not talk to the farmhouse or his driver or any one else regarding this arrangement. In keeping with Hauptman's advice Hazrara cancelled his rental car booking.

"There is no need to cancel your air tickets Mr. Hazrara" Hauptman had said.

The family along with Hazrara was transported in the armored vehicle that surprisingly had plush seats in the interior, to Huntington in Wales with Hauptman following in his embassy car.

Hazrara had no way of knowing all that happened later including the carefully arranged scenario indicative of a kidnap set up at his home in London for the benefit of anyone that may have wanted to find out. After the Hazrara family made it to Huntington, the particulars of the deal involving a multinational company in Uruguay were revealed to Nitin. He was asked to travel to a small town called Minas to meet the chairman of a multi-national company. Things were happening very fast as in a dream. Hazrara wished to travel to Minas with his family but was told that it was sufficient if he flew alone as otherwise it may raise unwanted curiosity.

"Mrs. Tavleen Hazrara and the kids could enjoy the hospitality of the president of Suleimania at Huntington where the embassy owned a huge manor house" Hauptman had said.

Hazrara wasn't convinced but was persuaded to go alone considering that the trip was not likely to be more than a week at the most. Hazrara now traveled with James Updike an Englishman to this small town called Minas in Uruguay. Updike made all travel arrangements and booked flight tickets from Bristol to Montevideo and then by car to Minas. Hazrara noticed that those working for the Suleimania Embassy seemed to be mostly non-Arabs, which was strange, as Suleimania was known to be a leading Arab nation. He turned to his escort Updike in a rather belligerent tone,

"What exactly is going on here? Why have you persuaded me to come to this Godforsaken town leaving my family in Huntington? What is the spiel? What does your so called first citizen want?"

Updike was nonplussed for a moment at the vehemence of the query but recovered quickly and shot back

"Why do you say something strange is going on here? Nothing in fact is going on here. We both have come here to close a deal which will see you become a very prosperous man beyond your wildest expectation, that's what my first citizen wants despite the fact that you are already a multi-millionaire of which fact he is aware."

"How come your first citizen of Suleimania controls vast properties here in England?" asked Nitin.

"It's quite simple really. England as a liberal monarchic democracy allows foreigners to have their bases in this country despite several men and women from abroad coming here as rebels to set up shop for their disruptive activities. In fact the British are proud to play host to rebels of all sorts and do not grudge them the facilities to do their work from Britain under the general immunity and protection of the British administration. In such a scenario our first citizen with his enormous wealth gets treated with respect and nothing is denied to him or his associates" replied James Updike.

CHAPTER 4

Huntington

"Mama I'm getting bored sitting here waiting for Papa to come and for the hols to start" said Shreya the sixteen-year daughter of Nitin and Tavleen Hazrara.

"We have to be patient honey, Papa has to close the big deal before coming back and you know it" Tavleen said with a bit of unease in her voice.

"I know how to brighten up things. Let's start reading the books I brought from the cupboard we had in Papa's den, the one he keeps his Yacht things in. I just bunched up a row of books he had in the bottom drawer and dumped them into my leather suitcase. They are sure to be a good read as Papa normally picks up the bestsellers as part of his collection and puts them in the den" said Shankar the darling son of Tavleen who was always trying to get his sister to marvel at his thoughtfulness in such matters. He wasn't disappointed.

"Well, well that's a wonderful idea. Let's each pick a book and read' said Shreya beaming.

Shankar quickly opened his leather case and took out the bunch of books. Shreya selected a book of short stories while Tavleen had her hands on a murder mystery by a famous English author. Shankar started sifting through the books to select one for his own reading when he noticed an envelope strong and thick of the type that came with its inside lined with cloth, a string neatly securing its flap by means of hooks on either side going circularly over a round leather washer sewed into the body to keep the contents safe and moisture free. There was some name written on the envelope that sounded Spanish.

Shankar took the closed envelope and was eager to see the contents hoping that they would prove exciting adding zest to the outing. He called out "Shreya, Mama just see what I found. It's an envelope perhaps from the yacht. May I open it please mama?"

"Of course you may do whatever you like unless it's a document concerning the purchase of the yacht by your papa in which case we must keep it safely till Papa sees it" said Tavleen.

"Oh, Shankar I'm so excited. Let's open the envelope 'chirped in Shreya

"The envelope looks pretty old but well preserved. I think this type of envelope was popular in London and other places in England some years ago. It may have belonged to the nineteen-fifties perhaps around ten to twelve years after the Second World War came to an end," said Shankar. The envelope consisted of a bunch of thin sheets of paper with a longish narration written in ink by what seemed to be a fine and artistic hand. "This looks mysterious and interesting. How is it that Papa never told us about this?" said Shankar addressing no one in particular.

'May be even Papa may not have seen this envelope which may have been lying between books that came in a bundle from the yacht' said Shreya.

"Give it to me and let me read it while both of you listen" said Tavleen taking the manuscript from Shankar. She was about to start reading.

"There is a caption written in bold letters here. I'm sure it's a private account of events maintained by the previous owner of the yacht on these sheets of thin paper" Tavleen said and looked at it some more.

"Look we better leave this to Papa to read because it's written by some person unknown to us" she said.

"Oh Mama it's even more exciting to read such a thing and Papa will have no objection I'm sure" said Shreya.

"We'll be able to brief Papa on this thing once we read it Mama. He will be pleasantly surprised that we found this and it'll be terrific if we find some new material that'll hold his attention" said Shankar. Tavleen decided to go ahead. She started reading.

'Record of my recent experiences'

"I George Douglas Hilton am writing this to record the recent events; some that could be deemed strange and inexplicable. I have wherever possible reproduced conversations as I remember them. I start with my visit to an interesting place. I have included background information wherever necessary.

March 1957 (No special importance to the date)

I was on a trip to the Isle of Wight across the English Channel in the spring last year and was holidaying on a small but well-appointed yacht that belonged to Senor Cordoz, father of my friend Miss Aleksandra. He was a regular visitor to our house in San Jose in California in the United States and knew my parents well. He normally came to England during the summer to spend a fortnight or more on his yacht "La Solaris". His daughter Miss Aleksandra or Sandra as she is usually called had asked me to accompany her to England for a short holiday to take advantage of the yacht's presence there. I readily agreed and both of us landed on the yacht on a Saturday. We met up with Sandra's brother Carlos and the three of us made merry, pub crawling and visiting dance halls and dining in exotic restaurants around Soho in London, returning to the yacht La Solaris at the beginning of each week for a two-day stay.

Sandra was an undergrad in the same university as me and was a student of the Arts and humanities while I studied the biosciences to prepare for graduating in medicine later.

We were both in our late teens when we first met. It happened accidentally at a party where I noticed that drugs were being offered around. It was Sandra and me that were the only two that said no and immediately a bond sprang up between us as teenagers that were not into cheap thrills.

No one felt that we had shunned the company of those that did drugs but just that we were different. None of our friends held it against us. We therefore continued to attend parties where drugs and other exotic things were done but managed to keep ourselves out, enjoying our own togetherness.

I have to mention here the huge hobby that Sandra and I had. It was the study of history, the past and particularly the rarely remembered history of civilizations, nations, cultures and traditions of much variety. They were items of great excitement to us. Sandra and I were avid readers and were excited to read books that brought out the details of events that happened centuries ago. We always enjoyed talking of history. Sandra would listen to my narration with great excitement as I described the majesty of the civilizations of Egypt Samaria and Mohenjo-Daro, they having come into reckoning after the earlier ones of Atlantis and Lemuria. I had excellent insights into the early Greek and Roman civilizations and their actions and practices apart from their conquests involving other countries and nations. I was telling Sandra how surprised

I was to read of the pagan Mongols led by Genghis Khan and later by Kublai Khan decimating many nation-states to establish an empire and the tales of Attila the Hun who almost laid Europe prostrate with his barbaric and unrelenting hordes attacking many European States and winning most of the battles. Then again there was the legendary 'Yama' on whom it was written, an eagle had placed the first Aryan crown over five thousand years ago in Bactria in the north of Afghanistan and much later the story of the phenomenal rise of the Arabs when Islam was embraced by vast populations in Asia and Europe and the eventual establishment of the famous Turkish Ottoman Empire. The exciting story of the Umayyad Islamic rule in Spain and the composite Spanish culture derived through its Jewish, Christian and Muslim inhabitants of various ethnicities including the Arabs and Berbers that stayed on even after its Christian re-conquest, impressed me no end. Sandra read about the wars of the crusaders and the heroism of many on both sides as also their brutality. Sandra apart from reading with me these books of interest also brought to me exciting tales from the Spanish conquistadores and their inroads into the Americas. Sandra was well up on the history of the Iberian Peninsula, particularly of Spain and its islands of Mallorca and Minorca and the pioneering spirit of her people giving rise to a composite culture that included an indomitable conquering zeal. Similar was the case with Portugal as one could surmise since Brazil which happens to be the only non-Spanish speaking country in South America, had Portuguese as the language of its people. Sandra was also keenly interested in the histories of great civilizations of the East like those of China, Japan and India and was eager to read ancient texts of those countries. The influence of Indian thought and culture was evident in most East Asian countries like Malaya, Thailand, Cambodia, Vietnam, Tibet and Indonesia. It was suggestive of how the early Indian teachers and nobles spread their culture including the great Buddhist masters and monks. She was surprised that Indian culture managed to survive elsewhere in south Asia and south East Asia while in India it was a different story. Constant wars among the many rulers that called themselves 'Maharajahs' had affected India's history. Every Tom Dick and Harry gathering a rag-tag army of mercenaries' raided India, pillaged and looted parts of that country with ease although these gangsters were ultimately robbed of their loot whenever they passed through Punjab the land of the five rivers as it then existed. Then there was the story of the earlier empires in India of the Guptas, the Mauryas, and the Kushanas (Kou-shi-Yang) all these ruling families having integrated into the ancient Indian caste of the Kshatriyas like many other foreign invaders that settled in India bringing their own cultures to get mixed in the cauldron of Rajput ancestry. It was interesting to read about the ancient Satavahanas, Cholas, Rashtrakutas and Chalukyas of the South and the empires of the north and how later the Moguls came to rule India and how their effort at integrating fully into the Indian culture failed because of their religion that demanded adherence to a codified set of laws that were different to those followed by the vast majority and how the Mogul rulers were ultimately led to demand and encourage the conversion of their subjects to Islam exemplified by Aurangazeb's intolerance in the end. The martyrdom of the Sikh Gurus and the 'Punj-Piaras' the five loved ones that were prepared to sacrifice their lives and the birth of the 'Khalsa' made a deep impression on Sandra.

Sandra and I certainly had an interest bordering perhaps on what could be termed as an obsession to know things from the past. We however were never prudish or bigoted to shun the here and now. It was therefore quite natural for the two of us to accept an invitation to attend a party being held at a friend's house in Chelsea in London where among other things some aspects of occultism were to be experimented with. It was just fun as far as we were concerned. Carlos as usual being uninterested at the time in anything other than an evening of enjoyment and dancing opted out and did not attend the party. It was at this party that we had met a strange personality. It was on a Sunday if I remember right. We met this extraordinary Youngman called Atulyaratna, a Muslim youth from Indonesia. He said that his name was of Sanskrit origin meaning 'invaluable gem' and that most names in Indonesia and the Indonesian language called Bhasa contained Sanskrit, a language of the ancient Aryan tribes that either originated or lived in India and spread to other countries. He said that Indonesia was proud of its Bhasa, the language of the region.

Atulyaratna had a strange story to tell. He said that in his village in Sumatra there was an old man who was thought to be mad and somewhat mentally retarded and was looked upon by the people around him with scant respect. One day this old man had an accident and rolled down from a height on a sloping terrain and was unconscious for a while looking dead. He was not seriously injured except for a bump on the head and some scratches on his hands and legs. He was however nursed back slowly to a state of consciousness and his injuries were attended to by doctors of the village. Suddenly it was noticed that the old man was talking normally and with a flair indicating deep knowledge and erudition. Atulyaratna went on to let us into an absolutely fascinating and fantastic story that took him the whole evening to narrate. The story that Atulyaratna narrated was as absorbing as the events in world history, except perhaps those legends of great prophets like Buddha, Mohammad, Jesus, Mahavira and others. Sandra and I were truly fascinated and intrigued by Atulyaratna's story and perhaps our upbringing had something to do with the neutral and non-biased manner in which we viewed it.

Sandra was the daughter of a super-rich father that spent money like water as the saying went. He had only two children, Carlos and Sandra. His wife had died when Sandra was three years old. He then shifted from Sacramento to San Jose to be able to spend more time with the children. Sandra was brought up rather strictly till she was eighteen and only then was she allowed a few liberties to meet and holiday with both male and female friends provided she was accompanied either by me or her brother Carlos. Religion as a rule did not figure prominently in the order of things and a dispassionate outlook was encouraged except that no sexual escapades were permitted and virginity was looked upon as a virtue in girls that needed to be maintained.

As for my background, I was born to wealth, the sole inheritor of an established although somewhat modest business empire with sales and returns running into millions. I had perhaps as some would say a pampered life. I was merrily carrying on in the university where my wealth was a closely guarded secret. I was good in my studies and had won the esteem of my peers and the affection of my professors, particularly of Dr. Barney who taught us mathematics and Dr. Croft who taught us Biology. I was like everyone else on first name terms with all my friends including the two professors whom I hailed as 'Paul' and 'Peter'. Additionally there was the one who taught us Chemistry, a Dr. Dasaka, hailed by the students as 'Surya' short for Suryanarayana, his first name. Being interested in India as a country of mystery, I was happy that there was someone like Surya to let me into the history of that renowned country of mystics and God-men. Surya rarely spoke of India but one could see that he was generous in his praise of her as a secular and responsible country that respected the beliefs of others and had given shelter to the Jews, the Zoroastrians, the Bahais and other persecuted communities allowing them to practice their religions and build their places of worship without hindrance. It was the country that greatly respected all religions including those whose followers exhibited aggressive evangelical zeal, Surya had said."

Tavleen Hazrara who was reading these sheets of paper to her children found that a few of the numbered sheets were missing, as the narrative didn't connect up correctly even though the general theme appeared to be the same. She felt that the missing sheets may have carried an interesting account of what the Indonesian youth had narrated.

"Let's have lunch and come back to continue the story" said Tavleen. She and the children went out to the 'Diner' for a quick lunch.

CHAPTER 5

Huntington

The 'Diner' was actually an out of use Railway compartment cleverly converted into a comfortable dining place like any normal restaurant, only not as wide, still maintaining the look of a dining car of a train on wheels. Tavleen and kids had a quick bite and returned to their manor house in Huntington.

Tavleen continued reading excitedly while Shreya and Shankar watched her keenly.

"Sandra and I landed in Delhi, India and were booked in an expensive hotel in the Vasant Vihar area. Our first objective was to meet up with Carlos who went missing after his arrival in India ten days ago. We first contacted the American Embassy where there was no information available. Next we went to Agra by car to see if there was any evidence of Carlos's visit there as he had expressed many times his keenness to view the historic Tajmahal in the moonlight. We drew a blank there as well. There weren't many options left except for us to go to western India and try and meet the old gentleman who had earlier been replying to the letters written by Carlos. As far as we knew, the name of the gentleman was Dr. Talpulvar living in his ancestral home in a small village called Pushkarwada in the state of Maharashtra in Western India.

"I wonder if Carlos has found some mysterious secret and had been following it up. Don't you think such a thing is possible given the penchant he has for solving mysteries all by himself?" asked Sandra looking at me in the mirror while tying her hair into a bun in our hotel room in Delhi.

"I doubt it. Carlos always communicated with me regularly to let me know all of the very minor and insignificant details and it is impossible to imagine that he would take off on his own to explore some secret or some mystery without first telling me about it. Sandra you know what I think, I think he is held captive. I do not want to say anything other than that even though I have a fear that the worst may have happened to him already." Said I to her in all seriousness and added "I am sorry it slipped my mind, I now remember he spoke with me on the night he left and said that he was going to India to meet this Dr.Talpulvar that lived in a village close to Nagpur in Western India. I repeatedly asked him if he was pursuing some hare brained idea of his to unravel some channel of communication to access the world of spirits like he tried to do while in Argentina. You remember how he used to hang around the Avenida Venti Settembre in Buenos Aires looking for a Spanish speaking person that he believed would accost him suddenly at sun-set, during the Easter holidays Don't you?"

Sandra did not say anything first, however she went on after a while

"I'm worried knowing that Carlos became a transformed person after that experience he had in London when he heard the voices of invisible men speaking of his close personal things that could not be known to anyone else"

"When did this happen"

"This happened on the day following the day we met Atulyaratna the Indonesian youth. It convinced Carlos it was a call from the unknown. It disturbs me"

I recalled that Carlos had not attended the Atulyaratna party.

Sandra continued

"Merely for the sake of information I told him of Atulyaratna and how you and I had been skeptical in the beginning but finally came to be stunned by his story".

"What did Carlos say?"

"Carlos was non receptive at first but a transformation happened after he heard the invisible voices. Carlos became a totally changed person. He became aggressive and demanding. He vowed to unravel the mystery of the old man of Sumatra even if it took him a lifetime." Sandra said.

I found some material concerning an Indian researcher called Dr. Talpulvar about human experiences at the time of death and other things. I told Carlos about it and he told me he wrote a letter to the doctor.

We decided that we should take up this line of investigation. Sandra agreed.

An Indian gentleman called Pramod Gadhvi, a reliable friend of professor Surya, was extremely helpful when I approached him in Delhi. I had brought with me a letter of introduction given to me by Professor Surya. Mr. Gadhvi filled in a lot of information about the Talpulvars of Maharashtra. I record below the words in general terms that Mr. Gadhvi had spoken or narrated on the subject.

"The Talpulvars are Telugu-speaking Maharashtrians like many others in Maharashtra having a 'var' at the end of their surname. Names such as 'sumanvar' 'Annamvar' 'Hedgevar' and so on could be mentioned as examples. It was believed that they had migrated centuries ago from the Telangana area ruled by the Nawabs of the Nizam to reside in the Mahratta country. It was indeed a common practice for many in one part of India to go over freely to some other part of this vast country and adopt the local customs and the language there. There were scores of such instances of mass movements. One would find Marathi speaking people in most southern states of India, some as descendents of the Maratha rulers and others that migrated purely for pursuing their professions. One would similarly find scores of families from Rajasthan in the Andhra region, keeping their original surnames except some who often attached it to a local first name. Similar was the case with a lot of Niyogis of Andhra who claimed their ancestry from Bengal, while the Dravida community traced their ancestry to the Tamil land in the south. All in all, there apparently was no animosity in the past at such migrations unlike perhaps in the present time when people I believe get deeply perturbed should such a thing happen. There is no doubt that this was a result of the destitution India has been reduced to, by foreign colonial rule, unlike the earlier times when India was rich and her people were generous and hospitable, each family properly housed and having enough and to spare," Pramod said which was a bit strange for me to understand and rather unrelated to the subject. He however went on with his narration.

"Pushkarwada derived its name from her people the majority of whom were priests that regularly conducted rituals at the twelve-year ceremony of worship called Pushkar conducted on the banks of the Godavari River at Triambak near Nashik. They traveled as a group and returned with enough earnings in cash and kind to provide them with a substantial reserve as a cushion to cater to any emergency, leaving their existing wealth untouched."

After this information conveyed by Mr. Gadhvi, I found out a lot more by probing into the Talpulvar legend at Pushkarwada by contacting the Maharashtra Association in Delhi. While the Talpulvars were not priests that conducted rituals at Triambak, they had been held in high esteem by the locals as enlightened persons that would uphold justice and fair-play unaffected by those occupying positions of administrative authority or those who flaunted their wealth as a qualification to have a say in the affairs of the locals.

I came to know the background of Dr. Talpulvar through Mr. Narvekar who knew the family quite well. He said

"Dr. Annasaheb Trayambakrao Talpulvar now in his seventies is unique in the sense that he is a fifth generation product of the family and had for his mother and grand mother ladies drawn from the highly erudite Sahasrabuddhe clan who spoke Marathi and were devout worshippers of Shiva that scrupulously followed the rituals and celebrations as ordained by the priests. Annasaheb married a foreigner; a sweet and graceful lady from England called Emma Nelson with whom he fell in love while studying advanced medicine and surgery in England after obtaining his basic degree from the University of Poona. Emma was Annasaheb's classmate at the College of advanced medicine and came from a Christian protestant family of Wimbledon near London. Annasaheb lived with his wife in England after marriage and both he and Emma practiced medicine for many years. Their only son Piyush the proverbial apple of their eyes was extremely intelligent and handsome. Tragedy struck the family when Piyush died suddenly after accidentally taking a dose of the medicine meant for his room—mate in the hostel of his school in Oxford. Annasaheb and Emma were shattered. After a year of extreme anguish they decided to leave England to settle and provide service to the poor in Annasaheb's ancestral place here in India. The orthodox family of Annasaheb's parents and relatives raised no hassles and Emma soon was a part of the Talpulvar family and came to be called Emma-tai by those around her and by a large group of her patients."

I learnt from one of the medical fraternity in Delhi who belonged to the Deccan area that a charitable trust was set up in the name of Piyush their dead son and both Annasaheb and Emma tai worked relentlessly to achieve their objective of educating the local poor without any charge and making sure that all requirements of cleanliness and sanitation were adhered to. Medical check-ups were free and those who wanted to donate money to the trust were free to do so but there was no demand or inducement of any kind. While Emma-tai was fully into the diagnosis and treatment of illnesses Annasaheb apart from his medical practice was into spiritualism and research on some strange aspects of the human mind, the nature of experiences and visions that people had under certain situations and pressures.

I was in two minds as to what I should do."

Tavleen stopped reading and put the manuscript down to let them retire for the night.

CHAPTER 6

Tavleen was excited and could hardly sleep that night. So were Shankar and Shreya. They got up early and had a decent break fast. Tavleen went back to reading the manuscript.

"Luckily the problem of how exactly Sandra and I should proceed to interact with Dr. Talpulvar

solved itself by a stroke of providence. Mr. Narvekar met me the next day and said

"As luck would have it I was able to talk to Dr. Talpulvar on the phone and he heard me out. I told him about you and he readily agreed to provide you with whatever information you wanted. He wished that you should personally discuss these things."

I thanked Mr. Narvekar for his kindness.

I decided to travel to Pushkarwada and personally call on Dr. Talpulvar. I mentioned my intention to Sandra who was eager to come with me to see if some information could emerge about her missing brother Carlos. We left for Nagpur in Western India by plane and made our way to Pushkarwada by taxi landing there at five in the evening. We had requisitioned a room in the circuit house at Pushkarwada and had left our baggage there, hoping to return back for the night. Dr. Talpulvar resided in a fairly large mansion built by his ancestors in the southern part of this small town. The building was of beautiful stone looking quite impressive and comfortable. Dr. Talpulwar was an impressively pleasant big built person who seemed to have an open mind on many subjects. Sandra and I were well received by the household even before we met the doctor couple.

Dr. Talpulvar explained his philosophy as regards his search for spiritual truths. During such research activity he said he chanced upon a strange technique practiced by some ascetics called 'Nava-Sadhus' roaming usually in secluded spots and hilly ranges or forests generally keeping themselves away from busy towns or villages that had sizable populations residing in them. "Their idea seemed to be to impart their technique to deserving persons after a conservative assessment of the candidate's integrity and intelligence" He said adding, "I had to literally roam around with them and behave like a nomad with no chosen destination. I had to eat whatever I could get or that given by kindly persons respecting my age and appearance. It was really tough and scary" He chuckled and continued, "Those fellows did not appear to be intellectually oriented. They looked like simple guileless people that would take things as they came trusting every word spoken to them by others. However there was some sort of a glow to their faces which no doubt came from inner happiness and peace."

"Did you manage to get hold of their technique Sir, whatever it was?" I asked.

"Unfortunately the answer is no. I did however come to know what it is and how it worked," said the Doctor.

"Did a person called Carlos meet up with you?" was my next question.

"Yes I think so. Are you not referring to a young man with receding hair with dreamy eyes standing rather tall at around six feet?" asked the doctor.

"Yes indeed. It is the person I'm referring to. Miss. Sandra here is his sister"

"He wrote to me earlier. I wrote back to say that if he wanted to know certain things he had to come to India. He came here recently and heard me speak of these strange people called Nava Sadhus. He pestered me to give details of the Nava-Sadhus and where they could be found. I tried to tell him how difficult it was to move around with them. He said he didn't care but that he wanted to meet them. I then asked him to go to Bandhavadurg not far from here. He left without telling me" the Doctor said.

Sandra and I were elated to know that Carlos was there earlier and right now was bound to be somewhere close by. Sandra was indeed keen to go in search of him straight away. I felt that perhaps going to Bandhavadurg might be the best thing to do. However I wanted to get to the bottom of what esoteric detail the Sadhus had known which they wanted to impart to any genuine follower of the path. I was more than sure that if we persisted in our query the kind doctor would certainly give us some important insight into this aspect. We therefore decided to stay on for some time to know more about the Nava-sadhus from Dr.Talpulvar."

Tavleen Hazrara continued reading the manuscript,

"Dr. Talpulvar went regularly for a long walk each morning. He did not mind me and Sandra joining him. After a bout of very brisk walking he would as a rule rest for about an hour at a circular platform built around a big 'shade-giving' tree and would restart the rigorous walking exercise in the opposite direction to get back. Sandra and I were relentlessly following up on our questioning to elicit maximum information on the Nava-Sadhus and their activities. Before he touched on the core of the matter, Dr.Talpulvar gave us an insight into the thinking of the Sadhus. He said that they were particular that a person should always live and act in the 'immediate present'. For them the present meant the interval between the minute that is now and the next four minutes that are yet to come. For them all that may have happened even five minutes previous to the immediate present at any point in time was the past and had no relevance and hence had to be erased from memory. They believed that a great Maharishi one of seven such rishis that received instruction from Shiva the Lord of cosmic energy was a deathless figure that lived in south India known as Agastya-muni. He is referred to as the founder of the 'Prana-yoga' and that he as its originator had exhaustively covered all possible ways of practicing the many kriyas involved in it. The Nava sadhus according to Dr. Talpulvar believed that Agatstya is blessed with eternal life and that Agatstya continued to appear along with two of his close disciples to all genuine practitioners of this yoga whenever they made a wish with great intensity to see him. He and his two disciples it was said manifested themselves as handsome young men despite their age of thousands of years. Dr. Talpulvar was not sure of the various powers the Nava sadhus possessed but was aware that they could disappear at will and reappear as and when they wished. He was he said an eyewitness to it. Sandra and I were excited to hear such things and said so to him. We also expressed our deep longing to meet the Sadhus and witness the miracle of disappearance. As for me I felt that such a thing was impossible considering the solidity and the complexity of human bodies. Sandra on the other hand was skeptical but not willing to negate the possibility of such a thing happening under some strange set of circumstances.

Sandra and I took leave of Dr. Talpulvar and proceeded to Bandhavadurg in search of Carlos. The good doctor had given a graphic account of the Nava-sadhus describing their capability to disappear and reappear at will.

"I can't believe that a human can disappear just like that. The Doctor could be wrong. It may be like what the magicians do with all the people in the auditorium uniformly observing a particular time in their watches and clocks as willed by the magicians using some kind of mass hypnotism."

"We can't be sure of anything just yet, Sandra. Let's see the things ourselves before passing judgment. We have to find Carlos first. That's our priority" I said trying to downplay Sandra's doubts.

"What about the past and the present and the five minute gap?" She asked.

"Well it's quite understandable if you closely analyze the issue. There are actions and actions and situations. If one wants to ridicule the concept one could say it isn't enough time to pee, to evacuate or have sex. Alright, but what about the big bang that created our solar system or a person dying or someone killing another, can we doubt that each of these could have happened within three hundred seconds? Time is relative. Even one minute may be the entire life span of an insect or a sub-atomic particle. Let's Just leave it at that"

The two of us reached Bandhavadurg the same evening which was a Saturday. The place was a small village somehow surprisingly neat and clean. There were rows of brick houses with wide enough lanes As far as we could see in the limited time, there were no shanties or slums and no one was begging for alms on the streets. Unlike some other places in India there was no one staring at us or trying to be overtly inquisitive. There was a bazaar with many shops and vendors selling stuff such as Indian sweetmeats, spices, fruits, mirrors, combs and what have you. We decided to go directly to the Bhairava temple that Dr. Talpulvar had mentioned earlier without bothering about anything else. On enquiry we were directed to a hill in the North-east part of the town where they said we couldn't miss it. Without stopping to buy anything in the bazaar, we walked to the temple site.

The temple was quite a big sized structure. It had a pond inside, in front of the main building. There was a stone wall all around the temple with two wide entrances one at the front and another at the south side fitted with thick heavy wooden doors. In the twilight of the evening we could see many lamps being lit. There were only a few men and women in the temple, some going round the main temple. The deity of black stone was decorated with flowers and something that looked like sandalwood paste. A priest with an impressive mien was conducting some ritual worship. Sandra was looking around to see if there was any one that looked to her like a Nava-Sadhu. Both of us were confused and had no idea as to how to go about finding these exotic sadhus. We decided to sit and wait inside the temple hoping for the best. We selected a spot at the pond just above the top row of steps that gave us a fine view of the temple's entry points. Sandra was depressed and showed it. We had come to the temple without bringing any food or water as we had not planned for a stay beyond a couple of hours at the most. We both were hungry and thirsty after sitting down waiting for three hours. It was past nine and the darkness was like a veil except for the flickering of the lighted oil lamps. The temple we knew would be closed for the night in the next half hour or so and we had no place to stay as we had not booked any accommodation in any hotel or lodge in Bandhavadurg. "Let's go into the main temple and see the deity" said Sandra. We got up to go but I said "What if the priest refuses entry for us?" Sandra wasn't bothered" What if they refuse, we just leave" said she. The priest was kind. He let us in. He recited some hymns while conducting ritual worship giving us holy water and fruit as benediction. "You seem to be outsiders. Have you got a place to go to?" asked he. We told him that we had no accommodation; he was concerned and affectionately allowed us to spend the night in his house and gave us a tasty meal giving us unexpected joy. The priest was a man of knowledge and was most helpful when we mentioned our purpose in coming to Bandhavadurg. "I've heard of the Nava-Sadhus but have not met them. You may be right about their miraculous powers. India is a country where nothing is impossible. We have such a lot of ancient literature that any obscure part of it, can grip one's imagination if one chances upon it." "We, Sandra and I, will be ever grateful if you could put us in touch with someone who may know about these sadhus."

"Alright, I'll put you in touch with a friend called shastri bhuva who could help you "He kept his word and personally introduced us to Shastri Bhuva.

Shastri Bhuva whom I would refer to as S.B. was a character, who though rather orthodox was yet modern and delightfully simple. He was keen to get us to meet a Nava-Sadhu without wasting time. He took Sandra and me to a lake about five miles away from the temple.

"The lake is of special interest to the Sadhus. They often come and sit on the bank and meditate" he said. It was indeed a long wait. We were in any case prepared with enough food and water. S.B. launched into an explanation of many spiritual exercises to attain higher regions of mental imagery to pass the time. Alas darkness thick and black of the night came upon us but there was no sign of any Sadhu. In utter despondency we left at midnight to rest at the lodge so kindly arranged for us by S.B. for a throw away price.

We were both disappointed and kept awake for most of the night. Towards dawn there was a sound which woke us up. We looked around and what a surprise it was to find a hand written message on a strange sheet of paper on our bed. After reading the message, both of us decided to return to London to prepare ourselves for the next course of action. We were sure that Carlos would have found Nava-Sadhus and was perhaps already with them. The cryptic message said "There will very soon be a great transformation through the spiritual mystics on our planet and there is an important role you two need to play. You both should therefore return to England without delay".

Sandra and I returned to London and are staying on board the yacht Solaris. Senor Cardoz intends to dispose off the yacht and return to the United States. We now await instructions from the source that sent us back from India."

Tavleen was nonplussed since the narration abruptly stopped and the page went blank after that.

Shreya and Shankar were both excited and were keen to find the missing pages if any. They knew that some pages went missing even earlier on.

CHAPTER 7

The next day, Shankar rummaged his leather suit case as also the books he had brought from the yacht. "Look here, there are some pages lying crumpled under the books, apparently written separately and missing from the main narration." He said and passed the sheets on to Tavleen. She had a look at them "These are from the middle. Something about the story of Atulyaratna" she said excitedly and started reading.

"Atulyaratna the Indonesian Youngman had held the audience in London spellbound with his story of the extraordinary change that came over the old man in a village in Sumatra, Indonesia. The old man that was earlier mentally retarded dull and ordinary with a pronounced stammer had miraculously become extremely coherent lucid and authoritative. He showed an awful command over the spoken language. When people questioned him about this miraculous change he was reluctant to provide an answer except to say that he was now a different person even though the body may have remained the same. It was ultimately the local Muslim Cleric that intervened and sought an explanation from the old man threatening to excommunicate and bar him from staying in the village if he did not explain. The old man insisted that he was willing to reveal the truth to only one person of his choice that lived in the village who could do whatever he wanted with it. The village council then decided to accept the condition. The council asked the old man to make his choice. The choice fell on Atulyaratna's father. The old man related his tale to him. The father in turn revealed it to the priest and the priest immediately put a stop to any further revelation saying that it is the devil's word and he wanted no one else to hear it. The excitement died down after that and the old man continued to be respected for his knowledge and the discrimination he showed in not revealing his secret to all and sundry. Atulyaratna however was able to get the old man's story from his father strictly on condition that he would not reveal it to others. Atulyaratna had kept his word while he was in Indonesia but he was under great strain keeping such a bizarre story a secret. His father had recently passed away and had left him in a dilemma. Being In London far from home Atulyaratna decided to finally share the secret story with a select group of young persons. That was how Sandra and I heard it that fateful day.

Atulyaratna said that the old man's assertions were fantastic and unbelievable and negated most religious beliefs held as gospel truths by the faithful.

"What were the assertions?" many that were present there had asked.

"For a start, according to the old man there are several powerful centers that control all living beings. Humans at the time of death lose their bodily identity as well as the attributes of name and form to pass through a series of stops to ultimately become tiny dots of transparent light capable of only one yearning that of receiving a pulse of energy from the control center that determines rebirth. The combined thought and memory bank passes on to the center that attracts it and stays there till it is either destroyed or given to a fresh 'body-mind combine' depending on the center. In the physical world unknown to us there actually are more dimensions that may be called the fourth, fifth and the sixth dimensions, unseen and unknowable by living humans apart from the three that we know namely length, breadth and height pervading all space. The old man did not count time as a dimension. These other dimensions are entered into immediately after death. Passage into the fourth dimension will result in an inconceivable boost in size while entry into the fifth will result in size change from the hugest to the tiniest speck. Entry into the sixth would result in a transformation into just a ray of light. Entry into these dimensions apparently is controlled by the centers.

The old man said he had lost all sense of his physical body but was conscious of utter peace and was not aware that he was dead. He was conscious firstly of a colossal hugeness and later of the smallness of the smallest spec inside an enormous envelope of space. After that a glow came over his consciousness and he could experience a sense of traveling at unimaginable speed first to one center and then to the other while his sense of peace stayed undisturbed all along. Although he was not aware of his body, he could at all times experience this journey that seemed instantaneous. He had no feeling of time in that state of absolute peace where the blissfulness that was being felt did not diminish. However he had seen or more accurately felt a glow of light and a thought occurred that he did not belong to the center. He did not react and continued in his state of bliss until he was violently shaken and awoke to find that his mental ability high, making the knowledge of things and ideas sit lightly on his mind. He also had a clear video like image of all that happened from his death till rebirth. He said that he had a visual image of a place where extremely huge sized beings were moving around who barred him from entering a particular place that he was not aware of and the next thing he visualized was that he was in the light glow as a tiny spec when there was a sound that told him 'Go back to a body waiting for you'. The old man said that it felt as though he was made into nothing at the time he was barred entry and that the spec that he was aware of was a different consciousness and the body he entered was not known to him earlier.

The old man was pointedly asked by Atulya's father "Do you know or remember who you were when you died?" for which the old man had replied that he could access many philosophical insights from memory but was not aware per se of the body he was previously in or the body he was living in at the moment. The old man said that the body aspect seemed unimportant and that the only important factor was his memory bank and the ease with which he could access it. When asked about how or what made him feel the process of travel without a body, the old man was non—plussed for a moment but collected his wits and replied "Physical movement which is a part of travel as understood by men and women with bodies is different from the awareness of travel that happened to me in my 'after-death' stage. I just knew," he said without defining what he meant by the word 'I'. While he could not define the person or thing that the word 'I' represented he seemed pretty sure of the experience of feeling. This is only the gist. Atulya spoke of many other things that the old man had revealed which I feel Sandra would not want me to record in a narration like this lest it be considered blasphemous."

Tavleen and the kids were more excited but had nothing else to read. The mystery of the strange message mentioned by Hilton seemed impossible to fathom. Nothing seemed evident.

"I'm sure the message is on the Yacht somewhere and I shall search for it high and low" said Shankar.

"I agree. Let's tell papa and go across to the Yacht" Shreya chirped in.

CHAPTER 8

Bandhavdurg

Carlos became a changed man after hearing the story of the Indonesian boy. It reignited his early childhood impressions of awe when people related incidents of mystery. There was a time when Carlos because of his deep disbelief of the refrain of those that urged people to repent for their sins and ask the lord to save them from hell saw the whole thing as meaningless. He was sure he committed no sin and the same was the case with all his family and friends. He went through his growing years fearing death and saw all men and women including himself as mere skeletons moving around and going through the routine of living out their lifetime ultimately to go back again to the grave. Luckily for him he met a mature practical person who guided him back to sanity. He learnt that by delving deeper and deeper into understanding how the world operated one is inclined to lose one's mental balance without in fact achieving anything. It would lead one into unending misery. He learnt that it's best to enjoy the pleasures available 'here and now' nurturing an attitude of carefree indulgence within limits. He did read many works of great men of religion and philosophy but was never convinced of what they said.

Carlos had corresponded with Dr. Talpulvar trying to gain insights into what life was all about and finally came to India to meet him at Pushkarwada to seek an explanation of what death was and what happened after death. It was Dr.Talpulvar who told him of the Nava Sadhus and their strange powers. He was advised that the Sadhus could be at Bandhavadurg.

Following the advice of Dr. Talpulvar, Carlos came to Bandhavadurg in search of the Nava Sadhus about whom the doctor had spoken highly of. He wasn't really sure that he would find answers to the queries he had in mind. He roamed around for nearly a week but wasn't successful. He chanced upon some middle aged bearded strangers that looked like dropouts from society merrily smoking some stuff called ganja perhaps like marijuana and getting high and subsisting on food and money offered by god fearing people of the place. He realized that these were not the Nava sadhus he was searching for. He kept his search going in the hope that he may ultimately end up finding them since his destiny had brought him to India which is their base. Carlos had not found the Nava sadhus but rather they found him. He went one day in search of them to the Bhairava temple at Bandhavadurg where by some strange coincidence he was accosted by an extraordinarily handsome youth who radiated friendliness and cheer. He seemed to be around twenty years or so.

"Aren't you the one searching for Nava sadhus?"

"Yes, how do you know?"

"I am one of them. You will find another like me at the river bank sitting down in deep meditation in front of a huge banyan tree. He is Kanaka. You can't miss him. You may tell him that Bala sent you. I'm Bala"

Carlos was astonished beyond measure and showed it. "Will he take me with him and teach me about how and why we are born on earth and why we die and who decides all these things."

"It's not so difficult. He will tell you many things. He also knows the story that made you come here."

"You mean Atulyratna . . ."

"Indeed, the Indonesian boy"

Carlos was speechless. It was bizarre and unthinkable that a person here in India knew all his innermost secrets.

"You go ahead and do as I said" Bala disappeared.

Carlos saw someone on the river bank sitting in the lotus posture with eyes closed in meditation. Carlos was a bit surprised to see that the person looked like someone from Europe. He felt happy that he will now get to know many secrets. Carlos could hardly wait to speak to this so called Nava Sadhu Kanaka. He waited for the Sadhu to see him first.

"Mr. Carlos, why don't you join me here" said the strange person opening his eyes. I'm not Kanaka that Bala told you about. I'm not even a Nava Sadhu. My name is immaterial but you may call me the Arrow. You wanted to know why people are born to eventually die and who decides these things, right?"

"Yes that's what I wanted to know. I'm not surprised anymore that you know my name. I'm sure you know everything about me and how I came here"

"Indeed, yes, it's all quite simple. What is needed is empowerment."

"Well let me first clear some of my doubts with you. I'm sure you will help me with answers"

"Go ahead. Remember I'm not a Nava Sadhu."

"For me it's all the same. You are one of the strange ones with some superior power and that will do for me."

"Alright. Ask me your question"

"Promise me that you will not hold anything back but will tell me what you know as I keep seeking answers"

"I promise. As I said I'm not a Nava Sadhu and Nava Sadhus are powerful humans who never speak falsehood. However I have no reason to mislead you."

"I consider you as my master and hope to experience truth whatever that may be"

"Fine. Please go ahead. Let me make it clear that I'm going to convey to you what my master told me. There will be nothing of my own in this"

Carlos was more than pleased. He was excited knowing that for the first time in his life he is talking face to face with a highly evolved human. Carlos had studied many great books of religion, philosophy and metaphysics earlier but had been utterly disappointed so much so that he had turned into a bohemian and an atheist. He had started splurging on the good things of life and was happy drinking dancing dating and generally having a good time.

Carlos started his questions. "I believe all things and events including birth, growth, decline and death of humans are pre-ordained, do you know who pre-ordains them?"

The exchange went on.

"While there are as many theories as there are strands of hair on my head, each belief is often claimed by its protagonists to have emanated from the Supreme Being. While we have statements by masters over the past many centuries on the basis of visualization or transcendental experience, there are others that are conceptually different. There is a concept I know of. It's the one my master expounded."

'Please go ahead".

"While many such theories are proclaimed true by the faithful, others, the so called pragmatists, pick flaws in them. My master says that the control mechanism of a living human which may perhaps be called the individual frequency is outside the person's physical body. He visualizes this to be connected in some non-physical manner to the brain circuit at one end and to a matrix far away from it at the other. He says this would explain one's out-of-body experiences like seeing one's own gross body from outside which happens when the brain's connections to the individual frequency and to the matrix undergo transformation, a temporary removal of the ego and the memory bank of thoughts."

"What then is death?"

"Before understanding the phenomenon of death, one has to see that death is inevitable when there is birth. Reincarnation happens selectively after death. This applies to all things in the universe from the biggest of planets to the tiniest of subatomic particles. It's better to call death as the end of an incarnation.

My master said that death is nothing but an out of body occurrence. A condition when the connection of the individual frequency to the brain circuit is severed while its connection to the matrix remains. Death happens to all, not only to the living entities but to particles of matter and all other substances in the universe without exception. The only difference is the time frame of the 'death—reincarnation cycle' which is different starting with a trillionth of a second for atoms or particles to billions of years for planets. Among those considered as living beings it could be a thousand years for a tortoise. In this cycle man appears to be in the 100 to 150 year range. Death happens when a combination of influences make it happen. We will come to that as we go along"

"What about reincarnation?" "Unless a special condition arises when the individual frequency is severed from both the brain circuit and the matrix resulting in the non existence of that individual frequency, a human or for that matter any entity has rebirth. The non-existence happens when it becomes a part of the core of the matrix as the core draws to itself all the disconnected ones. The matrix is a realm of Supreme control operated by a unique universal frequency. Incidentally there are many matrices. There are those that control matter and those that control life as we earthlings understand it."

"I seek your pardon but I've always strongly believed that no human can ever know the truth which is in a dimension unknown to him or her and utterly impossible to fathom, given the limitations of a human's potential to perceive through the triangle of sense organs, intellect and intuition. Your master would certainly know that" Carlos said.

"Hey, permit me to go on with my master's concept. The next major question is about this connection between the brain, the individual frequency and the so-called matrix. How are these connections made? How are the connection between the brain and the so-called individual frequency maintained or severed? How did the matrix happen and who or what made it happen. You will be impressed by my master's answers whether right or wrong. He is most consistent".

"What does he say?"

"He says growth after birth is related to programming that selectively determines one's evolution. The elements of male and female energy Yin and Yang which is known as Shiva and Shakti in India get activated when fertilization happens. According to him the human body is an entity continuously connected through its porous transparency to various other bodies in the cosmos and is under their constant and continuous control and itself controls other bodies through a series of unique vibrations."

"Are all bodies inter-dependent?"

"Yes and the connections are through a medium not apparent or discernable by any human intellect or intuition. The trigger or stimulating agent of controlled frequency of a living body or Prana as mentioned in Sanskrit lore is connected to the matrix of universality encompassing all frequencies."

"What do they call it?"

"The matrix, particularly its core, is called by different names by theorists one such being 'The Realm of Light' in English and 'Vibhasa' in Sanskrit. This matrix contains the male and female attributes that enter into each individual frequency to control and sustain activity. Prana has within it 'Chaitanya' or liveliness, which in simpler terms could relate to vibration. All these taken together may enable the matrix to perform and hence they form its component parts."

"It seems pretty simple, more like what we learn in science fiction?"

"My master says that life is a miracle with living bodies floating in a continuous envelope of air and other gases which again are a conglomeration of elemental particles on our planet 'Earth' that is spinning and rotating at great speed with rays of energy entering and leaving through spaces and through pores of skins affecting each of the three main sheaths that a living entity has, namely the gross body of outer skin and other astral bodies that are in the realm of individual frequency. The entities unaware of this fact carry on merrily believing in physical attributes of shape form and environment.

"Let me be quite frank. I am very skeptical. I somehow feel that all this as propounded by your master could be mere idle imagination within the limited parameters of a human's mental activity which is basically chemical in nature. Therefore I insist that the real thing cannot be and will never be known to your master or to you or me or to any human being"

"Let me continue. I contend that the master has defined the components of a workable system. One cannot say the system is true since our capabilities and senses as humans are severely restricted and our vision is blemished to an extent that one may say that it is impossible to know the truth."

"Who controls us, does your master have an idea?"

"Perhaps that is why the master says that we humans had to put in place concepts of a universal father or mother or a combination of both, creating and ruling over their creation. The idea was to make one believe that a 'father-God' or a 'Mother-Goddess' or a combination of gods or other similar deity figures created this universe of all things seen and unseen." "How are we to address them?"

"They who at every millisecond or less of earth-time, monitor every sin we commit and love us and forgive us our sins provided we pray and sing their glory and live and act according to their commandments and follow the guidance so lovingly given by them over thousands of years through their angels, prophets and messengers or by themselves directly taking birth on this unique planet called earth which as we all know is but a tiny and insignificant sphere-shaped object in space, one of many such objects that are like specs of dust or dots in a vast boundless cosmos."

"This is rather simplistic"

"Yes but a widely held belief. This concept of the one God or many Gods controlled uniquely by a main God principle might ultimately turn out to be the absolute truth. Who are we to say yes or no? The fact is that we humans cannot be sure of anything that lies beyond our capacity to perceive or understand, the master said. It could be that a very simple answer exists and that God could be a man-like or a woman-like figure of immense power that controls everything in some mysterious way. Or perhaps we as part of the matrix ourselves create the world and sustain it by our will. It may also be that God is formless, all pervading with no beginning or end and so on so forth."

"Very convenient indeed, indeed"

"Thanks. The fact is that no human normally wants to make sacrifices to know the truth unless it is for his glory and for his unlimited happiness here and now or in another world of which he has no real knowledge except what has been given to him through channels he considers holy. The human also wants to be free of pain, physical disability, poverty, sexual impotence or infertility and illness apart from worry and stress, all of which are the ills one encounters in life in this world. Anyone who removes his or her pain in a jiffy or removes one's stress or poverty or sexual malaise becomes a savior worthy of elevation to the status of a 'miracle—performing super-being' and the religion or the path of action laid out by this super-being or by his followers becomes a sacred belief to be nurtured and spread.

"Okay, what is the harm?"

"This commitment becomes so potent that one would be willing to kill those who oppose or contradict this sacred belief in any way. It is a fact that a large percentage of people follow and fight for this or that religion more out of a strange fear rather than out of any conviction arrived through a process of self inquiry which may be the case with only an enlightened few, says my master."

"I agree, there is the fear of infamy, fear of deprivation, fear of being left out, fear of so many other factors and the ultimate fear of punishment in a horrendous zone called 'Hell'. For many life is a routine, a continuation of one's family traditions, beliefs and rituals providing a comfort zone already in existence at the time of one's birth and nurturing him or her till death. However tell me more about the master's theory"

"I'll tell you. I know you are hungry. Let's have some food"

"I do not want to stop our interaction. I can stay without food"

"That won't be necessary' said the person and in no time produced hot food that came into the plate that was lying on the ground next to him. Carlos stopped marveling at miracles anymore

"Now let's eat" said the person.

The food was delicious

CHAPTER 9

Bandhavdurg

The exchange between Carlos and the stranger continued.

"What do you define the so called ego of 'I' as understood by the spiritualists?" asked Carlos.

"Spiritual teachers discuss the concept of the identity of 'I' in the human context as to whether it is the gross body, the mind, the intellect or the soul etcetera. The common refrain is the example of a person calling the parts of his or her body as 'my body',' my hand', 'my face' 'my lungs' and so forth signifying that he or she is the possessor of, but not the body or its parts referred to. The argument is perfectly valid. However let us take the example of someone saying "I ran', "I walked", and "I kicked". In this case what does one mean by it? No one says 'my legs ran' or 'my hands slapped' and so on. In other words whatever the body does or the mind conceives or feels is expressed by using the word "I". In other words the totality of the body with all its systems and supports is the "I". This is one way of thinking. Some say that there is a witness in us which is a part of us that is ever present from birth to death, before and beyond birth and death that is the soul which is indestructible. The best thing is to leave it since we are not provided with the ability to go beyond the limitations of our sense organs of touch, taste, sound, smell and sight." was the stranger's reply and he went on further to say

"To let you know a great secret I have to tell you of my own experience with my master. My master touched my brow one day and asked me to describe what I saw.

What I saw was exceedingly strange and awe-inspiring. I do not know if it was a dream or if it was real. I saw an enormous stretch of terrain between two huge distant snow-capped mountain ranges. There was no access through the mountain ranges making it impossible to reach there unless one flew over the glaciers. I was there but did not know how I got there. In this relatively vast flatland there was a huge area glowing with light. One could notice an unending screen of light as long as the eye could focus apparently closing in on itself as it spread over to the left and to the right in all directions, its vertical height seemingly disappearing into outer space. Millions of small dots, crosses, circles, asterisks and other unfathomable symbols were flashing on to this unending screen at random. They were going off the screen and reappearing at speeds that could be described as unimaginable by human intelligence. Positioned on lines passing through the center of this complex matrix of glowing color screens, were rows of huge spatial cylinders, each cylinder made up of clusters of colored sparks that shone like diamonds, rubies, sapphires, emeralds and other gems of rare brilliance. These cylinders of light that seemingly disappeared into the sky were constantly rotating on their axes at considerable speeds flashing symbols on to the screens all around. The whole scenario was inconceivably bizarre and mind blowing"

"It may be a hallucination that was induced in you by the master" said Carlos.

The stranger smiled and said

"Be patient. The master spoke to me after this vision. He spoke slowly and clearly and said "I'm glad you saw this mind blowing spectacle which is beyond description by words known to you or me or to any fellow human. I say that there is a logical explanation of what you saw. What you saw was one of the control centers on Earth of non-human non-limbed creatures. The matrices controlling the lives of humans and limbed creatures are in higher dimensions which for some reason are separate from those of all other species. It is a self-contained self regulated system that is similar to an administrative hierarchy as we know it, controlled by a number of main cores of the main matrix each responsible to monitor one of the directions for ensuring the working of the total system. Each symbol on a similarly enormous screen located in a higher dimension has a role to play in controlling the activity of each single human and in registering continuously on the screen at a dedicated space every action from the first breath at birth to the last breath at death, monitoring all activity, recording it and the resultant gain or loss of the glow factor specific to that human. The control center is constantly bombarded with sparks of light from planets and spheres around its axes hitting the glow spots of each individual symbol methodically affecting the glow quotient which in turn adjusts the individual's action at all times throughout life because of its connection to the individual consciousness of the person. In other words planetary influence is an important factor"

I asked my master to reveal to me the matrix configuration.

The master explained thus

"The core of each matrix is a part of the Universal core capable of drawing unto it all the loose and floating individual matrix cores under the eternal laws of relationships between the individual and the universal. Now you have seen the effulgent light of the matrix, can you guess where it comes from? The light screen and the symbols are a complicated configuration controlling the life of each entity represented by a symbol that stays on till the individual awareness exists. Once merger happens the symbol is altered and becomes attached to another individual awareness. However the record will be present in the ever flowing continuum that may be viewed by any empowered being. It may be worthwhile to look at the vast and enormous life in the non human context comprising birds, animals, insects the crawling and the creeping ones, germs, bacteria and a million other as yet un—identified entities all throbbing with life, consuming other life for food to prolong their own existence. Somehow most humans believe that all non human life is soul-less and insignificant and has been expressly created for human benefit and to keep man well provided with meat, eggs, milk, leather, various necessities, cleansing compounds, bacteria, essences and so on. Our view of the non-human life is skewed. In fact it is quite important and does play a unique part in the regulation of human life. The light screen has specific symbols each of which connects an entire group of a non limbed or non moving species to the matrix and controls it. How the glow factor operates and in what manner it controls and records all activity is a matter I cannot explain nor do I know it in my present human form. I have an intuitive concept that the glow factor is color oriented.

Now coming to the presence of light, we know that God appeared as a beam of light without any form or shape according to the scriptures. The famous Ten Commandments were given by such a manifestation of light as described in the Old Testament and as 'Divya Jyothi' or divine light in eastern languages. Light therefore is an attribute of the super human and light it is that made the matrix. It is not possible to explain it any further since the human intellect is not equipped to understand it"

Said the stranger turned to Carlos with eyes filled with kindness "I'm telling you all this as an introduction for you to transcend a dogmatic mindset that most humans are equipped with.

Carlos in turn posed a query "Hearing your revelation I am very confused. You should tell me of what your master said about who decides the death of anything"

"It is a closed cycle and death happens automatically in accordance with the laws that operate the matrix. There are various aspects that control the glow and radiance factors of each unit and death is controlled by the radiance factor. Death happens when the factor reaches its minimum value. Planets, other bodies as well as the actions and repercussions of the specific unit, affect this radiance. The glow factor on the other hand determines the behavior pattern particularly in the case of humans. *It is necessary to remember that you and I are nothing but specs of life or life—force occupying human bodies presently. When you or I are there the bodies we occupy have life. When you are not there the present body is lifeless. You enliven whatever body you enter. You as life or life—force have no death except ultimate merger with the core of the matrix giving up your separate identity.*

Saying these words the stranger touched Carlos with his finger on the forehead. The next thing that Carlos saw was something he could not comprehend. He shouted in great excitement

"I am speechless. I now realize that we, you and I, are actually physically in sight of the matrix. How did we get here? Is this what the supreme power is all about? Is it so easy to de-materialize and re-materialize our physical atoms? What is destiny? Who decides it? Who programs the minds of sentient beings? Questions aplenty indeed! I know. I also know that you will provide me the answers in a manner that will make me understand and that you will later safely get me out of here even though it matters little whether or not I get out once I know the secret of these things."

"This matrix is an earthbound one handling only the non-human non-limbed aspects of the world mass. There are such ones in the fourth dimension which is beyond reach for you and me unless there is empowerment.

Just remember that you have forced me by your genuine quest to bring you here. However I've to first take you through a story covering some years. You have to carefully see the scenes as I narrate and show what happened. You are now empowered to see an audio visual presentation of things as they happened. I have mustered the facts from the continuum that I had talked about earlier.

Incidentally I was born on earth in Italy and am part of a large circle of people from all religions and nationalities committed to the welfare of the world which in fact is one unique family inter related in numerous ways. You will understand how I finally got the empowerment to reach here comparatively recently. The fact as to how I came to acquire the crucial knowledge to reach this place is a story that starts with my meeting in Katmandu with my master. You will see the past and the present all mixed up but in separate positions. The future is not there to view as it requires a different level of empowerment that I do not have and thus cannot initiate others. The matrix having given you a glimpse of its form will now move out of your view and can no longer be seen. What you will now see is an audio visua show of what has happened over the last few years apart from what could be relevant to you and me"

"I'm prepared"

"You will see your sister Sandra and George Hamilton who is now your brother in law. While we were talking, a certain amount of time in years has passed by, which you couldn't notice.

Your sister Sandra and George had come to India searching for you and were asked to go back to London which they did. They are both spiritual masters today. Your father is back in San Jose. He sold the yacht to an Indian businessman who owns it now.

While I narrate the past to you somewhat like a story-teller, you will see the actual action scenes. You will see a colossal worldwide endeavor by misguided humans to decimate all men and women that believed in spirituality. This movement was instigated, organized and executed by a powerful coterie of armament manufacturers enormously rich and dealing in trillions of dollars. Their trade of trillions they felt was threatened by spiritual men and women. They were scared of the idea of unity of all religions and in the doctrine of re-incarnation propagated by the spiritualists. They set up a worldwide network called the 'Cleansers'

You will see the murder and mayhem perpetrated by the so called cleansers.

You will see the intense positive regimen the spiritual masters tried to follow for defeating these so called cleansers and bring them round to appreciate spiritual values but having no success.

You will see the final confrontation that came from the spiritual masters and grand masters and how they with their combined power and their cooperation with the greatest scientific talent and resources available after the Second World War put in place a solution that was unique. I will not elaborate.

You will now witness the story with different locations and scenarios as it actually happened. The past and the present could well be jumbled up. I myself may be part of the scenes you witness. There are personalities reincarnated to deal with just such a situation. Here you go. I'm with you and will guide you. I'm saying this since I was a part of the struggle that ultimately succeeded in making our planet a better and a more peaceful place."

Carlos was flabbergasted with this development. He was surprised to learn that his father had sold the yacht. His entire outlook had changed and there was no ambiguity any more. He started seeing things which he had missed out on, during the time he was with this marvelous super being called the Arrow.

CHAPTER 10

Katmandu

Carlos started hearing the steady narration in the friendly and intimate voice of his mentor the Arrow while viewing the action scenes as if in a movie. He was amazed at the clarity of the narration and the scenes. It started with the Arrow's voice "Carlos this is your good friend the Arrow. Now listen carefully to my narration and see the action".

Prior to his initiation Daniel Stone was a brilliant scholar with wide knowledge of history, philosophy and Philology and had for years delved into the mysticism of the East and the West. He had come to Nepal in his thirty-second year with the intention of seeking spiritual experience many westerners talked about. He was keen to meet up with someone that could lead him into higher levels of mental concentration. One day as he sat looking at the temple of Pasupathinath in Katmandu he chanced upon a passerby that smiled at him in a way that touched him. It seemed as though the eyes of the stranger radiated unconditional love. Daniel returned the smile and fell into a conversation with the middle-aged person who spoke in broken English. Daniel felt very happy for no particular reason.

"I see you are guest in Nepal"

"Yes. I come from very far"

"What you like to see?"

"I want you to show me a God-man."

"Me, I can take you Maharishi very old saint man" said the man in broken English.

"Right now or sometime later today may be"

"This evening if you are wanting"

"Does he speak English?"

"He speaking English very well"

"Take me to him this evening"

"Show me your living place. I will come at six"

Daniel took the man to his room in the modest tourist lodge at Janakpura. The man refused to eat or drink anything in the lodge despite Daniel pleading with him to accept the hospitality.

"I'm eating only one time a day in early morning and nothing eating after that."

"Well, I'll wait for you here"

"I come back at six" the stranger left.

The man came on the dot and Daniel went with him and met the saint. He was flabbergasted to see such a healthy 'saintly—looking' person who was stated to be over ninety years old. The sturdily built saint was looking fresh with no major signs of advanced age except his white hair.

The man who escorted Daniel went to the saint first and spoke with him. He came back and took Daniel to meet him. Daniel felt a sense of peace and harmony in the presence of the aged saint.

"I knew that you will come to see me. You have studied much and have spent a lot of time looking for spiritual experience. You stay here with me and you will attain what you are striving for. You should inform your mother in Philadelphia. She is waiting to hear from you." said the saint.

Daniel though surprised showed no outward indication but simply nodded his head.

"There will be many more surprises for you when you stay with me for the next three years. Do you wish to see your mother and talk to her?" asked the saint.

This was way beyond Daniel ever imagined possible. He became very humble and said" Yes indeed. I'd love to see and talk to her."

"So be it" said Dharmaprgjna the saint.

Suddenly all went dark for Daniel for a split second and his mother appeared in front of him looking happy at his sight. He did not know whether he had gone to his mother in Philadelphia or if she had come to him in Katmandu. He talked to her eagerly and fast and she too talked.

Suddenly the scene changed and Daniel was back where he was in the saint's presence.

"Thank you. I will stay here all my life" said Daniel bowing to the saint.

"We'll see about that. You're staying here for three years. That's for sure "said the saint.

That was how he had become a member of the Ashram run by the saint.

The saint gave a new name to Daniel. He called him 'Nishta Pragjna'.

This was the third year of his stay in the Ashram.

One day the saint asked Nishta Pragjna to sit with him. There was a silent exchange of information.

'Yes, you got it right. I have decided to alter the scenario. I feel that there is a task that I have to concentrate on and complete as soon as possible. I am to travel to another sphere of great importance to initiate a new line of selfless beings to protect the earth. This is to be done quickly. I'll be gone on the evening of the fifth day from today. I want that this Ashram should continue."

"Where do you intend going master?"

"I'll be leaving for a destination in Tibet".

"I shall follow your instructions and from my heart I thank you for everything you taught me as my master and Guru. I know that you can manifest to me in the form that I'm familiar with at any time. I only ask you to do so whenever I call you. I'll only call you in an emergency"

"Done. Let me now tell the rest of the inmates"

"I'll call them to come over to listen to a special message you want to give them"

"Do that. Except for you and Chandra, none of them are able to receive my message by mind mail. I have already spoken to Chandra."

Chandrapragjna alias Chang Wu was senior to Nishta by ten years having come to live in the Ashram from his native China.

"Chandra will take over the ashram and you should go back" said the saint

"Where do you want me to go back to master?" Nishtaprgjna asked,

He was sad that not he but Chandra was being chosen to run the ashram.

"You are to be the leader in a great struggle that is coming up. You will use all your powers and lead an international team of grandmasters. A Youngman will come to you two days after I depart. He will tell you his story. Keep him with you and assign to him the right type of responsibility"

"What is the person's name?"

"Alberto. He is from Italy"

"I will take care of him"

"One other important matter remains. A master will come for you on the fifth day after I depart and he will take you to the teacher"

'What teacher? I do not have anyone other than you"

"It will all be crystal clear as the teacher will instruct you by mind mail before he meets you"

Things happened exactly as planned. Nishtaprgjna assumed his original name of Daniel. It was amazing how many extraordinary skills and powers he had attained in a short span of three years thanks to the love and affection of the saint who transformed him into a spiritual super master. With his original identity back in place, Nishtaprgjna now awaited the arrival of the young Italian and the spiritual master that would come and take him to the teacher.

On the second day the young Italian arrived and met Daniel. He narrated his story

"I am Alberto Rimini from Italy, from Milano in fact. My people are jewelry makers using gold chains, gems and beads. I lost my family in a fire accident when I was still a teenager and was distressed and depressed. I met a peculiar person who explained to me the futility of desire and ambition. He created in me a deep thirst to know the truth, the secret of life and death. He encouraged me to listen to men and women who are into spiritual practices and meditation. He said that I will come to know many things and one day I will reach unknown spheres beyond our known dimensions. I am now committed to travel worldwide hearing the saints and great men speak. I travel from place to place, from country to country and am ever eager to know the truth from the yogis, fakirs, saints, shamans or whoever I chance upon. I survive on frugal food and drink bought with money left to me by my parents which is quite substantial. I seek out modestly priced hotels, motels, lodges and so on for my stay. One will find me listening to discourses by men of knowledge wherever I go.

When I was in London I came to know about Kosmica, a body given to the spread of spiritualism. I studied psychology at Victoria University purely to understand the behavior of humans and the way their minds analyze the implications in a given situation. In my early adolescent years I was incessantly troubled with powerful negative thoughts about life and its purpose, death and the horror of it. I chanced to come here to this Ashram five years ago and stayed for two years with the great Guru. He made me a different man. At his instance I resumed travels and attended many discourses. I now know my purpose in life"

"Say no more. I too know your purpose in life. I also know how you have helped out those that met with danger because of their spiritual orientation" said Daniel

"The Guru said that you will assign me my work"

"Yes indeed. You are to be with me all the time and accompany me wherever I go. We will talk about other thing later"

Alberto was very happy to hear that.

Daniel now awaited the spiritual master that would take him to the teacher.

CHAPTER 11

Lewes, Outer Hebrides

Carlos continued to hear the narration and viewing the action scenes guided by the Arrow.

It was a magnificent office with the chairman's chambers at one end of an impressive hall in Lewes, Outer Hebrides

The principal secretary Mrs. Pamela Goddard in the anteroom was attending to phone calls on the chairman's exclusive line. The phone rang.

"This is the hotline for Sir William Witherspoon. How may I help you please?"

"Pam, this is Victor. Put Bill on for me, will you"

"Just a moment Sir" Pamela connected the line to the chairman Sir William.

"Hello Victor, this is Bill. What's up and why the urgency?"

"Things have gone haywire. I won't mention names but four countries are canceling their orders and more will follow I'm sure. Billions worth of armament stock—fighter planes, tanks, missiles, frigates, destroyers, field guns and transport vehicles and a thousand other items will stagnate creating problems. There is no clause in our huge multinational conglomerate's various contracts for compensation for cancellation of part quantum if conveyed on time which you already know. We are badly jammed as we are always ahead in production schedules never ever expecting this sort of a development."

"Who's responsible for this sudden move for god's sake?"

"I can only guess. One of the countries involved had a spiritual biggie traveling and lecturing about afterlife, reincarnation and all that ballyhoo. Perhaps the powers that be are mellowing towards universal peace and a non-conflict mode in inter-state relations."

"What makes you think so? Listen, could be this is just a one time thing with no connection to the spiritual abracadabra and perhaps things will be normal and hanky dory pretty soon"

"Bill, I sure wish it's so; but my boys round the world have sent me reports of a huge spurt in yoga practice, mysticism and nirvana through love, peace, brotherhood, fellowship and that sort of thing. It worries me. I have indications pointing to likely cancellation of armament orders by six other countries including Indonesia amounting to 42 billion at present market rates. We'll be digging our graves if we let things drag on like this. The latest rumors are that this biggie the so called spiritual grandmaster has sent out his band of disciples to brainwash the ruling juntas in many more countries"

"Well, that does put a different picture on the issue. I'm with you and fully agree that it signifies grave danger. Victor I do not want you to hesitate. Just go ahead and do whatever it takes to stop this nonsense. Utilize the underworld and our special teams round the world to snuff out the menace. Approach all contacts in the defense ministries of these countries and swamp them with lolly, lots and lots of it. I'll work on the political angle to bribe through. Also work on getting a top spiritual biggie on to our side. Work on his ego." Said Sir William the world's most feared Armaments tycoon.

"Roger. As you know we already have an extensive well knit organization spread throughout the world. They have unlimited funding facility and will come in handy for what we intend to do. They have thousands of armed men on the payroll willing to jump into the fray on orders from me. We have recently roped in a powerful group of people from all corners of the world to be led by a strong American fellow called Miller who has a huge corporation with branches round the world. We will now join hands and form this body which I will name as 'The cleansers' I'll keep you posted. As usual I'll ensure that no one traces our actions to the armaments group" Said Victor Abrahamson, Chairman 'Imperial Trading International' a proxy company controlling enormous supply chains of armaments worth hundreds of billions of dollars with production units in many countries.

Suddenly orders, instructions, requests, entreaties, started flashing across the globe. The message was clear. "Eliminate all mystics and spiritualists no matter what background or religion they come from. Use force in any form to any extent and do not repeat do not spare any of them. It has to be a holocaust without exception."

CHAPTER 12

Cairo, Egypt

Carlos kept listening and viewing, while the places of action kept changing across the world.

"How strange and what a mess. Is the world coming to an end Allah permitting?" asked Mohammed Abdul Gaffoor a Sunni Muslim cleric of Alexandria in Egypt.

"Why do you ask?" questioned Aamir, the seventy year old daily help in the Noor Mosque in Gazabieh neighborhood in central Alexandria.

"I've been reading the news in many papers. In Istanbul and Al-Qahira, some of our brethren have died mysteriously. Report of attacks on Maulvis and Allah's men of the Sufi sect in Indonesia and the Sikh and Hindu priests in India, Nepal and other places appear regularly in the papers"

"What about those from Israel and the Christians?"

"They are equally targeted all over Europe and America. Even the Buddhists are not spared in China, Thailand and elsewhere."

It was true. There were gory deaths in several parts of the world due to attacks by unidentifiable brigands. Simultaneous attacks in Britain in the cities of London, Birmingham and Liverpool were synchronized to happen within twenty to thirty minutes after sunset at three different locations. The Death toll was estimated at over ninety men women and children, those attending discourses and practice sessions of spiritual masters. In Argentina a monk of Asian origin and his disciples were attacked and twelve persons died. Buddhist mystics in Tibet were subjected to atrocities and some were burnt. In Israel two Kabbalah mystics were kidnapped and no trace was found of them.

There was panic and people weren't sure what was happening. The Administration and the police in all these places were clueless.

The religious leaders were equally confused and dismayed. The Catholic Church and other Christian churches condemned these attacks. The Islamic clerics spread across the globe were divided in their reaction. Some deemed it was Allah's way of dealing with blasphemy while others were shocked that the Sufi sect of Muslims and others were being wrongly targeted and murdered. The Jewish, Buddhist, Hindu, Sikh, Jain and other religious heads strongly condemned these attacks and urged the governments of the various countries to bring the culprits to book and deal with them with an iron hand and stop this massacre.

CHAPTER 13

Himalayas

Carlos continued with the Arrow's audio visual inputs with enthusiasm.

The young looking bearded person with a commanding presence known simply as 'the teacher' started speaking to a modest group of serene yet happy looking men and women drawn from all parts of the world in a cave in the snow capped Himalayas bordering Tibet, India and Nepal.

"Though born into Hindu, Christian, Islamic, Jewish, Sikh, Jain, Buddhist, Zoroastrian and other traditions, we have over the years evolved universally applicable thought processes and physical activities that had in their own wise way, good—heartedly countered the ritualistically organized religions and made reincarnation an acceptable concept. The process took hundreds of years. The ancient Mexican shamanism delving into the spiritual mysticism of experiencing the Supreme "is-ness" the Jewish Kabbalah, the Al-Ahd and Sufi traditions of Islam, The Rishi and Guru traditions of the Hindus and Sikhs, the Christian Cabala and Assisi schools and the many Buddhist versions have shaped our spiritual vision and practices infusing into us the unflinching determination to love everyone and to hate no one. We have among us masters with rare powers that appear strange to the multitude.

It is now time to recount the suffering the world went through in the not so distant past.

The deadliest Second World War killing millions in Europe and Asia got over a decade and half ago after the unfortunate and gruesome use of those unholy atom bombs that wiped out and maimed thousands in Japan apart from the millions killed in battle and in the gas chambers in Europe.

I am sad to tell you that another great struggle or war will happen soon to cause widespread murder and mayhem. I can see that it has already started."

The teacher looked at the audience with deep love for a moment and continued

"Those spreading harmony and brotherhood like us are under attack. Spiritual awakening is under threat to be blocked and the masters and grand masters are targeted to be killed to create fear in the people.

These negative forces cannot be allowed to succeed. We shall safeguard the practice of spiritualism of the highest order on earth. Surely this great battle for spiritualism will matter the most since man has gone on to develop enormous destructive forces that will proliferate and hold the world to ransom. Spiritualism is the only force that will save the earth from total annihilation. All of us my dear friends shall do our bit in ensuring the welfare of all beings on this planet now and for ever. We will spread out to teach the power of self—belief and the greatness of all religions and belief systems that ultimately lead one to a state of blissful existence through meditation, prayer and yogic power"

There was a sense of satisfaction among the men and women that heard the teacher who they lovingly considered as their spiritual guide and mentor.

Those present reaffirmed their desire, their determination and commitment to continue the good work despite the dangers that they may face.

Groups were reassembled to go forth and spread spiritual values and practices as also to train men and women giving them proper knowledge and power to teach and inspire the common citizens towards the ideal of 'one world one family'.

After a while a master approached the teacher and said "I've brought him with me"

"I know. Let us meet in the inner cave" the teacher said.

The teacher accompanied the master and met Daniel. Daniel touched the teacher's feet "You have already conveyed your message to me through mind mail. I await your instruction"

"The core group is here and you are to lead it. All decisions will be yours. I will now give you a detailed picture of the 'realms of light' that decide everything"

The teacher then gave a bird's eye view of how the universe is run and the role the core group is to play in furthering the cause of peace and harmony to undo the malefic actions of the bigoted organization working against the practitioners of spirituality and spiritual values.

CHAPTER 14

London

Carlos now could with the Arrow's help view and hear people discussing in London.

"Did you see him?" asked Mr. Thornton.

"No. I'm going to, very soon. People have told me about his powers." replied Mr. Scott.

Both of them had met up at the Century Club in London and fell into a conversation sitting in the members' room sipping scotch on the rocks'.

"He I am told is not very old but can talk like a scholar on any subject."

"I believe he has rare powers."

"He is thought to be close to Kosmica"

"Who is Kosmica?"

"It's an organization of spiritual seekers with centers in most countries"

"Very interesting. I'm sure he is thought of as an incarnation of some great soul that started manifesting its powers"

"There is a major controversy. A section of society is trying to portray the person as an incarnation of the devil. They are even demanding that he be arrested and confined to a secure prison thus cutting him off from the multitude."

"Perhaps wanting him to be burned at the stake as in the olden days."

"Very true"

"I hear he has received death threats from religious fundamentalists the other day"

"How sad and ridiculous indeed"

"Does he perform miracles?"

"Well it depends. When needed he is said to have materialized objects from no where. He is also believed to be capable of becoming invisible staying at the same place or instantly appear at a different place hundreds of miles away"

"It must be acknowledged that he has superhuman powers"

"But I believe he says that anyone can do all these things once he or she follows a path of meditation, and Yoga under proper guidance and with dedication"

"Perhaps he is right".

Similar exchanges were taking place at several centers where a number of spiritual persons were being targeted by organized groups.

CHAPTER 15

London

Carlos guided by the Arrow, heard and saw how the ordinary spiritual people were coping with the cleanser antagonism by ensuring self protection in more practical ways.

One such effort made in London showed systematic orientation of training and subsequent action.

Carlos was made aware of how it all started.

An advertisement in the classified columns of the London Times read "Wanted a sincere healthy educated young male assistant proficient in any recognized martial art trained up to black belt level or higher to travel with an elderly gentleman to any part of the world. The candidate must be proficient in English and should be capable of understanding at least one other European language such as French, German, Russian or Spanish. The perquisites include free lodging and boarding plus a salary. A monthly remittance could be arranged as needed to meet the expectations of a middle class family in the United Kingdom or Europe. Interested candidates may contact Mr. Mason at . . . ." An address and phone numbers followed.

Pradip Hemant Bose aka Prabo aged twenty five, fit and full of beans and a martial arts enthusiast had been struggling in London to make ends meet after his master's degree in psychology. He never forgot his days living as an orphan in Bombay being known as 'Chinku' to all and sundry. He could never forget the old gentleman in Bombay who happened to help him get out of his life of a street urchin. He it was who took pains to trace Chinku's roots.

"Do you know that you were orphaned when your parents Hemant Bose and Madhobi Bose could not be found after the Howrah Bombay Mail accident that took fifty nine lives? You survived and were admitted to Ganesh Home & Orphanage in Palghar when you were three years old. The orphanage closed down when you were five"

"I have been lucky. I may have been brought to Bombay by some kind person" was all that he said hearing his sketchy biography.

The old gentleman became rather fond of Chinku in the weeks that went by. He would meet Chinku twice or three times a week and spend an hour or two each time talking of many things.

One day he asked Chinku "Look, will you go to school if I took care of your needs of food, clothing and shelter?"

Chinku was overwhelmed at such unheard of kindness and was most happy to say yes.

Life changed completely for Chinku after that. The old gentleman made Chinku adopt his original name for admission to a well known school. Chinku had now become Pradip Hemant Bose. He graduated in psychology and came to London for higher studies thanks to the trust funds of the old gentleman. He however wanted to stand on his own legs and not keep drawing from the trust grants.

Bose after his master's degree in psychology was presently assisting the rehab board of the British Immigration to work with immigrant asylum seekers particularly in counseling the poor and the lonely. He decided to keep his effort temporarily aside for the study and research for a doctoral degree.

Prabo as usual met his friend Adrian Nathan seeking his company that made him forget his travails at least temporarily

"Aren't you looking for a job Pradip?" asked Nathan

"I certainly am. Where is it?"

"It's in an ad in the times. You seem to meet the requirements. You have to phone and find out. Let me see, maybe I can do it for you'

"I am of Indian origin and have an Indian name which may be a disqualification."

"The empire is no more. I don't think that these things matter now. Yet there's no harm trying"

Nathan did so. The advertiser a Mr. Mason lifted the phone and spoke.

"I have no problem with a person's name or nationality as long as the person is qualified for the job in all other respects."

It was agreed that Prabo should meet Mason that evening. The meeting went well for Bose. Mason was much focused and appeared to be in his sixties. Bose was grilled over the next three days of interviews and was able to come up to Mason's expectation. Bose was given the job.

"I want to train you to perform. You know me now. I do not believe in half measures. You shift your stuff to the hotel Horizon tonight. You are to be present in a track suit at my place by early morning tomorrow, say at 8 A.M."Bose was given a room on the third floor of the hotel Horizon and commenced his training with Mason in right earnest. The first month was spent in rigorous martial arts training imparted by specialists. Bose, a Karate black belt learnt split second responses to aggression from any quarter as also the most effective way of using karate kung-fu Tae-Kwan-Doe and aikido techniques to bring a person down with minimum effort and maximum success. Mason was a hard task master and made sure that Bose imbibed the essence of the training given each day by the experts specially engaged for the purpose. After three months Mason had a special session with Bose to explain a lot of things."One of the reasons I selected you so quickly is because you have a very good background with knowledge of yoga and meditation techniques which I consider desirable given the fact that you were well up in all other requirements that were essential. I can now tell you that I had interviewed quite a few candidates in five countries in Europe before I advertised in England. I had short listed some but selected you and no one else. You will now be selecting a team of six to seven others in less than a month. I have notes on the short listed candidates that you could use"

As per plan a team of seven strong men and women was formed with Bose taking up the onerous mantle of leadership. This was achieved quickly as Mason had already short listed the eligible ones from those interviewed by him earlier. The team apart from Bose had two British nationals, one Italian, two Germans, one Chinese and one Indian all of them healthy and strong men and women in their late twenties or early thirties with a variety of skills with black belts in the martial arts. The three girls one each from China, India and Germany were Sui Wu, Shalini Rathod and Hilda Meyer presently living in Europe. The men were Mark Crawford and Timothy Graham from Britain, Frederick Stoldt from Germany and Ricardo Rossi from Italy. They went through a course of intensive training for two months. The team assembled at the hotel Horizon in room 318 where Bose stayed. Mason made a special appearance. He addressed them.

"We have come together as a team with Bose at the helm for an important assignment that has a lot to do with the welfare of humanity. There are such teams in other parts of the world thanks to the foresight of a spiritual guru and Grand master of British lineage in London. Our main purpose is to counter the powerful forces unleashed recently by the so called Cleansers that are threatening to wipe out those undertaking spiritual practices and endeavors. I will now let Bose explain the aspects more fully"

Bose took over the floor.

"I have to elaborate a bit more. Spiritual practices and beliefs create and maintain peace and harmony among men and women irrespective of their religion, social status, color, education, age or aptitude. The cleanser forces are negative, very powerful and economically strong with unlimited finance at their disposal. They are headed by unscrupulous men that believe in maintaining the status quo of chaos and inter-religious conflict in the world and are scared of people losing two of the most potent traits that drive them today namely their ethnic and religious identity."

"I have a question" said Hilda Myer

"Please go ahead and ask"

"Will it not be right to say their inherent and natural desire is to dominate the weak, the poor and the dispossessed?"

"Correct. Propagating a belief in deathlessness of the spirit and in reincarnation would in their view unite humanity and enhance harmony. It will naturally eradicate the desire to go to war either to impose one's religio—political ideology or racial superiority on others whom they consider ignorant. It all adds up to show their desire to create and magnify human conflict."

"For whose benefit?" asked Sui Wu.

"The idea is to lead to war and it's after effects of repression and torture. They intend to subjugate and rule, in the bargain making trillions of dollars boosting corporate enterprise involved in the production of arms, nuclear weapons, ammunition, missiles, fighter jets, submarines, destroyers, aircraft carriers, and a plethora of systems and related equipment on a colossal scale."

Mason took over the floor

"All of you as members of this team 'B-7' are here to protect our mentors and friends identified by their belief in spiritualism. We have been given an important task to immediately undertake. I am detailing

Mark, Shalini and Ricardo to join Bose in this. I have booked additional rooms in this hotel"

The three of them stepped aside standing next to Bose.

"Bose, Mark, Shalini and Ricardo are to monitor the activities of the spiritual masters through Kosmica that is actively involved in the spread of peace and harmony through spiritual teachings yoga and meditation exercises. They will travel to various places around the globe as decided by Kosmica to protect the masters and the members and would not hesitate to use force if all other peaceful efforts fail"

"The rest of the team is detailed for an equally important function."

A look of excitement took over.

"Hilda, Timothy, Frederick and Sui are to join a Mr. Bainbridge who will tell them what to do. Mr. Bainbridge is also the personal aide of the grandmaster Parama. The team will operate in London and other centers in Britain" said Mason.

CHAPTER 16

Huntington

Carlos was made aware of what happened to Nitin Hazrara and his family.

"Madam we have arranged a small outing for you and the kids. Kindly be ready by noon so that you reach the place in time for a sumptuous dinner, our Secretary Mrs. Timberlake will escort you there. Our chairman Mr. Miller has arranged for his wife Mrs. Wilfred Miller to join you with her teen aged daughter Maureen for lunch tomorrow." Said Richard Smith addressing Tavleen,

"Where are we going?" she asked.

"To Brighton Madam, a lovely and immensely popular holiday resort" said Richard.

"I've been there many times and so have my children. We would rather stay on till Mr. Hazrara gets here. Please convey my regrets to Mrs. Miller. I'll speak to her if you wish" said Tavleen.

Richard left saying "I'll convey your decision to Mr. Miller, Madam"

After two days he received orders from Miller to see that Tavleen and the kids were brought to the Isle of Wight saying that Hazrara had gone directly to their Yacht and that he wanted them as he was arranging a grand party to celebrate his successful signing of a huge business deal and had invited the Millers as well.

Meanwhile Hazrara was back in Huntington

"I'm sorry but it's the truth. Your wife and children left the house without telling us or asking us to accompany them" said Richard who was entrusted with the care of the Hazrara family in Huntington. "We have no idea as to where they are now. It's best to wait at least till this evening before jumping to conclusions. For all we know they may be coming back home within the hour" Hazrara was shocked beyond words and stood there in stupefied silence not saying anything. He and Updike had hurriedly made it to Huntington after closing the deal in Zavros. Updike was upset too and showed it. He shouted at Richard "What the hell do you mean by saying you don't know where they are. The fact is you lost them. They are not objects but invaluable guests entrusted to you for safe keeping and to provide security with service day and night every single day and you have failed and put them in danger. Do you understand the enormity of your callousness?"

Richard tried to answer but kept mum seeing the anger in Updike's eyes. Nitin Hazrara was nonplussed. "Let's get out of here right now. I don't trust these people. It appears there's some sinister design and we are being given the wrong information. I know my wife and my kids. They are not fools to go away just like that. It's utter nonsense. Look here Updike, You get on to your bosses in London and get some answers before I blow my top."

Updike contacted his boss in London, a man called Miller.

Miller said "Updike listen, I want you and Hazrara in the Isle of Wight without delay. Give my regards to Mr. Hazrara and tell him that we are all happy that he signed the big deal. His wife and kids are safe and are being escorted to the Isle of Wight by our trusted guards who were able to get them away in time from a group of thugs who were trying to take them as hostages for ransom."

"Why would any one want to do that?"

"Perhaps they knew that Hazrara had a two billion dollar deal all signed and tied up"

Updike made immediate arrangements for travel. Hazrara was literally seething with anger and frustration realizing his helplessness and worried to death about the safety of Tavleen and the kids. Updike assured him that his family members were all safe after their rescue from the kidnappers and that they were proceeding to Ryde where their yacht Solaris was anchored in the Isle of Wight.

Tavleen and the children meanwhile were being driven to 'Ryde' in the Isle of Wight after disembarking at Cowes from the ferry. They believed that Nitin was already there and was throwing a party to celebrate his business success.

CHAPTER 17

New York

Carlos guided by the Arrow had a glimpse of the Cleanser set up.

The man known as Oscar Miller spoke to an assorted team of scientists, doctors and others that sat round in an office overlooking the river.

"Gentlemen, an international council headed by me is in place for vigorous and immediate action against our opponents. The other members of this council are James Warner, Nikolai Dimitriev, Julio Fernandez, Reza Amanathulla, Joseph Bartholomew, John Balasingham and Bill Mackenzie. They are all here. This council will have the support of the heads of all our branch offices worldwide. The council will co-opt others as necessary from time to time. The council will report to the High Command and follow their guidance"

Miller continued;

"As you are aware, I have been told by our benefactors and the high command to take good care of the London businessman Hazrara and his family. All four of them will be dealt with as already decided once Updike's mission is completed. Updike incidentally does not know anything and has been given the job of leading Hazrara through that Arab deal. The family meanwhile is being transported to the Isle of Wight and arrangements are in place there to deal with them as planned."

"Aye, that's a job well and superbly, handled Mr. Miller. I congratulate you on behalf of the entire team" said James Warner a psychologist and an important member of the recently formed council.

"Why the Isle of Wight may I ask?' interposed Brian Black.

"The family's yacht is moored there and lots of surmises will be made by the investigating police officers handling the case which is good for us," said miller.

"Good thinking indeed. I hope all of you gentlemen are with me on this. May I remind this congregation of what Miller and I were able to put together by way of authentic information on the danger that the Hazrara family posed to our command control system" Warner said and went on to elaborate "You are aware of the enormously powerful 'High Command' that is presently operating from ninety two countries and Island States that keeps us fully employed and busy. Our orders are directly from the head quarters. We are to eliminate the Hazraras who may be the empowered ones to destroy the high command and much else that I have not yet been told of. An attempt is to be made very soon to enter a secret domain of which I have no knowledge. We are here not to ask why but to do and die, as the saying goes."

There were nods of approval from the men and women that crowded round the rectangular table in Miller's posh office.

"What will happen to the Hazraras?" Asked James

"They will be killed and their bodies thrown into the sea next to their yacht "Miller said.

As an afterthought he added "There is going to be a major confrontation when we take the fight to the enemy. Major preparations are underway and they expect full cooperation from all of us"

CHAPTER 18

London & Marseilles

Carlos now began to see his sister Sandra and George and their progress. He could hear the narrative and see the action at different locations thanks to the Arrow's guidance.

"There's no time to lose. Let's join the others forthwith" said George Hamilton addressing Sandra.

"How time flies. It seems like yesterday that we left India and returned to London. Father's return to San Jose after the yacht was sold and the disappearance of my brother Carlos have stopped bothering me after we met Parama who initiated us into this wonderful life of spiritual grandeur. I am with you. Let's go."

Parama was the one in London a mystic with great yogic powers. When George and Sandra came back from India to London, on the second day a letter arrived for them from a Mr. Kimberly inviting them to join the 'Kosmica' a cosmopolitan group of spiritually minded persons who had their weekly meetings at an address in south London. Sandra was excited. "I'm sure this is not a coincidence. We are being guided by those who sent us back from India"

"I feel the same."

They went to the meeting and their lives changed in many ways. The person known as Parama was an Englishman of extraordinary presence, a yogi radiating positive energy all around him.

He told them to get married so that they could fulfill an essential requirement before being taken into the fold of spiritual leaders assigned to deal with certain matters that are vital to safeguard the welfare and safety of humans.

They did so without much ado and integrated themselves into the group. George and Sandra were then asked to get back to America and await further developments. They were told that they would be required to work on the organizational details of an event of which they would be informed well in time.

Events started happening at speed from then on. The cleansers were succeeding in their mission of eliminating spiritualists of all hues irrespective of religious persuasions mainly because of the widespread network of organized and armed killers they had working for them. The body of men and women that Sandra and George were part of was doing great work in disrupting the killer gangs of the cleanser brigade. Regular training camps at isolated locations were being held to improve the spiritual power and dedication of the participants. Confrontation was skillfully being avoided by a spy network that sent out alerts about the intended places of attack planned by the cleansers. As a part of the non violent strategy the cleansers were being fed with wrong intelligence inputs about the places where spiritualists were to be meeting.

Later in the year there was a request from Kosmica for Sandra and George to travel to Marseilles to meet with Parama who was camping there.

"Sandra let's go and meet up with our great guru' said George. He had already booked tickets by Air France from San Jose to Marseilles.

They arrived at Marseilles at night and came to know through the local Kosmica office that Parama was giving a lecture the next day at the World Peace convention being held at the University Hall. They decided to attend and call on Parama after his lecture. It was a conference of eminent men well versed in the sciences and humanities. The grand master Parama was giving his address. "All life on earth is a part of the vast network of matrices, an endless continuum of light with seven colors each representing a category of beings. Miniscule spots of light each spot identifying an embodied life are in the continuum. Each and every body or thing has three essentials, namely life, death and reincarnation so called for lack of any other suitable definition. The past, present and the future positions of each body or thing are evident for one who can observe them in sequential order., All three namely the past, the present and the future each corresponding to a given time frame along with the relevant images are recorded and present in these continuums in the precise sequential order in which they happen. Each continuum associated with its matrix is endless existing for millions of earth years without any lack in its potential and is visible to any intelligence that reaches the third realm. From this realm one could detect the differing visages of each life or thing as incarnated in separate modules of time-space. Thus one could see two, three or more images of the same entity, giving the illusion of seeing it in more than one place at the same time. Let me give you an example.

Physicists are mystified by the behavior of particles, the same particle being present in more than one place at the same time. How can that be? They ask. We should reconsider the problem with the knowledge that a particle's identifying feature such as a face for instance is unseen and un-see-able with our instruments. We only see the path and surmise the presence of the particle. The time difference between the death of a particle and its reincarnation could be so small as to be unfathomable by any instrument that a physicist has produced till now. One should then appreciate the inadequacy of our observation based on our equipment as presently available that may not be having the degree of sophistication needed for accurate measurement. Under the circumstances it is clear as to why the same particle appears at two or more places at the same time. We must remember that non limbed entities such as particles of matter and lower life forms such as worms, insects, and bacteria and so on are born, die and reincarnate in the same dimension on our planet whereas humans and the limbed entities pass through other dimensions before reincarnation and are part of an imaging continuum that erases and restarts imaging after seven consecutive incarnations of each entity.

The phenomenon may be explained by a further and more apt example. Let us say that a person called John lived on this earth from 1800 A.D. to 1880 A.D. died and reincarnated as Chang and lived between 1880 and 1970 and so on. John and Chang will both be found in the continuum occupying different places. For some one observing from the third realm in 1965, it will appear as though the same body namely that of John reincarnated as Chang is in two places at the same time, unless the observer can detect the difference in appearance of John the Englishman and Chang the Chinaman and the difference in the time-frames between their separate existences. In other words we need to consider three things. Firstly the difference in the time-frame of that body's existence in the continuum, secondly the difference in physical appearance of the body existing in separate locations in the continuum and thirdly the time frame of the observer who is able to see both locations of the same body at the time of observation.

It is true that in the universe, all laws apply uniformly to all entities whether it is a star or an atom. As explained earlier, there is a dimensional shift in the case of reincarnation of non-moving and non-limbed life forms such as particles of matter and worms or bacteria etc., which go through a transformation process in the same dimension for re-incarnation whereas the limbed ones go through the fourth and other dimensions prior their re-incarnation. It is also true that frequency of vibration is the measuring stick that determines the form and nature of each body. Now a scientist who observes the phenomena of a particle being in two places at the same time is in fact seeing the particle and its reincarnation in the continuum thus mistaking the particle to be in two places simultaneously. Yet one more thing to ponder is of the nature of vibration which is a bit of a mystery and may differ somewhat from the classical definition of physical science as conceived by humans. It could be a strange mode of vibration that controls or establishes the nature and shape of bodies and things.

I now thank the organizers for giving me this opportunity of sharing my thoughts with you. Thank you."

The grand master Parama concluded.

Just then an Italian youth Alberto Rimini of exceptional grace approached the grand master and whispered something in his ear. The grand master got up and quietly left the hall with him.

Once out of the building, the youth said "We only have twenty minutes before the syndicate eliminates the family"

"Time enough to do what is needed. Let's go."

The grand master held the youth's hand and both of them disappeared.

Sandra and George were disappointed that they were not able to meet up with Parama. However, a message was received by them soon after.

"Parama knows you are here and wants to see you both at your place after a couple of days. He will come to you in the evening" said Safina a member of the Kosmica to Sandra and George. They were both extremely happy to hear this.

"May peace be with you" said Parama to Sandra and George on the third day, meeting them at their lodge in Marseilles. George and Sandra bowed and shook hands.

"I have an important assignment for you. You are to proceed to Spain and establish yourselves in Madrid. Kosmica will help you in all matters. You are to set up a communication network and select the site and support logistics for an important gathering of spiritual masters who will meet somewhere in Spain. You have a time frame of four months to do it.

"It'll be our pleasure and satisfaction to carry out the assignment to perfection" said Sandra.

Sandra and George went back to San Jose in the U.S. wound up their establishment and headed for Madrid in Spain flying with the Iberian Airlines. Sandra was particularly happy "I can now revisit all the wonderful places beginning with the Palace and the Prado museum in Madrid" said she to George. "The Prado museum in Madrid, the Cathedral in Seville and the Alhambra in Granada, are landmarks of significance apart from the palace. Another place is Catalonia which is unique considering the contribution of Gaudi's architecture. I would like to start with a walk down La Rambla, then, see the Sagrada Familia, and the Barcelona Cathedral" added Sandra.

"We have time for all that, thanks to our assignment which involves a lot of travel"

Said George and read out a piece from the write up on Spanish history which said

'The Barcelona area of Catalonia has served as a crossroads throughout history and the city has taken on the flavors of the invading cultures. Carthage, Rome, the Visigoths, the Moors and France (under Charlemagne) at one time claimed this area and each of these cultures left lasting impressions on the city. Under Spanish rule, Barcelona was not always been a good place to be, but of late, the city has revitalized and taken a leading role in Spain's growth and modernization.'

Sandra could not agree more with this assessment quoted from the write up.

The local Kosmica found a place in downtown Madrid that could serve as an office for George and Sandra who traveled to various parts of Spain and to the islands nearby trying to set up the communication network of activists for Kosmica vastly improving on what was already there.

Sandra was excited to re-visit her favorite spots in the Mediterranean with beaches located in the south of the country as well as in the northwest. Spain had a great number of landscapes, including forests, salt marshes, rocky bays, mountains, as well as cities from the medieval era, rivers and mountain ranges. It also had various castles, palaces and other marks of the early richness of Spain. Work progressed at a fast pace for Sandra and George. The membership of Kosmica increased many fold with Sandra convincing the selected people at different places in fluent Spanish the benefits of spiritual practices. At the behest of Parama they selected the Mallorca Island as the place where the world spiritualists could hold their conclave. They went ahead booking the main venue in the huge tourist resort of 'Palou de la espana'

Sandra brushed up her knowledge of Mallorca's history. She read the information given in a book which quoted the historical aspect and said;

"Evidence of other people to settle on Mallorca has been found and includes findings of tools made from animal horns and pottery that are from around 1000 BC. Other evidence to prove this time is in the towers shaped like cones (Talayots). They are a periodical feature for around this time. They are sited in the south of the island at capocorp vell. These were named The Carthaginians.

The Next people thought to arrive were Greek and Phoenician traders. This is where it is thought that the name Balearic came from ballein, which is a Greek word for sling throwing! The Carthaginians worked in conjunction with the sling throwers to fend off the Romans over time, until the Romans eventually took control in around 123 BC.

If Mallorcans were to ask, "What have the Romans ever done for us?" The answer would be that they built the first towns and roads and also introduced Christianity to the region along with its first civil structures.

In the tenth century the island began 300 years of Islamic Moorish rule after the Emirate of Cordoba assumed power. Mallorca had a very contrasting 300 years in these times, as holy battles for power would commence between Muslims and Christians. Eventually, however, due to the considered location of the island between Islamic Spain and Africa, trade and agriculture flourished.

In 1229 King Jaume I of Aragon and Catalunya invaded the island of Mallorca. The Mallorcan Emirate stole his ships and this enraged him. Moorish buildings were destroyed and with this he set up an independent Kingdom of Mallorca. He built the Palma Cathedral. He was a very good governor. Well ahead of his time he would do all he could to assist traders in the region as well as give equal rights regardless of religious beliefs. After he died King Jaume left Mallorca along with some of his other provinces to his son Jaume II. Pedro IV of Aragon landed in Mallorca in

1349. He was jealous of Jaume II and so claimed control of the island for himself.

Mallorca's traditional language up to the 18th century had been Catalan. This was then replaced with the Castilian variation of Spanish. However during the Napoleonic wars Mallorca still saw more than its fair share of Catalan speaking refugees. 19th century life on the island of Mallorca was a tough time for the island with Famines and droughts throughout the century. As the island saw advancements agriculturally along with a new rail network and increased communication with Spain there was a feeling of revival of the Catalan culture."

George was excited about the forthcoming spiritualist convention at this beautiful and historic location. He and Sandra went ahead planning by finding accommodation for the many participants all of them masters and grand masters of different backgrounds. Arrangements were being finalized for their creature comfort and for providing spaces of silence for meditation and introspection.

Unknown to Sandra and George there were some people monitoring their activity in making elaborate arrangements for what appeared to be a forthcoming get together for around two hundred people at Mallorca. This information was passed on to the cleanser monitors confirming what they already knew.

CHAPTER 19

Isle of Wight

Carlos was now viewing with interest the life and activity of the Hazrara's family shown by the Arrow.

Nitin Hazrara was dismayed at the turn of events and rued his unfortunate decision in London to go along with the machinations of the Arab Embassy's emissaries instead of keeping the family's holiday schedule. He was traumatized thinking of the danger he put Tavleen and the kids into. He silently prayed to his family deity as a devout believer, asking for protection and for ending his and his family's present predicament.

Updike and Nitin arrived at the Isle of Wight by a specially chartered aircraft. As they disembarked Updike was totally dismayed when Hazrara was forcibly taken away by some goons who said they were doing so at the orders of Mr. Miller.

As the goons got Hazrara into their station wagon and started moving out, a curious thing happened. The vehicle stopped and the goons got thrown out one after the other as though by some invisible power. The vehicle started moving again by itself with only Hazrara in it, scaring the wits out of him. "Do not be afraid. I am a friend and am driving this car even though you cannot see me" said a message recorded mentally by Hazrara. "Your wife and kids are in grave danger and we have to save them" the car gathered speed. It finally stopped at Saint John's bay, north of the Island's waterfront area at Ryde. "You may now get down and wait. Your wife and children will be brought here by your enemies who behave as friends of your unsuspecting wife. I will deal with the enemies and release your people. You are not to interfere in any way whatsoever. You should take your people into the vehicle and head for a place called Yarmouth where a special launch is waiting at a private jetty to pick you up and take you to Falmouth. Some one else will guide you after you leave here" Hazrara's mind listened.

Things happened as predicted. A luxury car arrived with Tavleen, Shankar and Shreya escorted by a well dressed lady besides the chauffer who looked muscular.

"Madam, Let's proceed to your yacht where Mr. Hazrara, the Millers and guests are waiting" said the escort addressing Tavleen as they got down, leading them to a white painted speed—boat tied up at a berth a couple of hundred yards away at the quay. Things started happening all of a sudden. The chauffer collapsed in the car screaming loudly leaving the lady escort shocked. She rushed back to attend to him, leaving Tavleen and the kids walking towards the boat waiting on the quay to carry them to their yacht. Shankar and Shreya were excited and happy that at last they were rejoining Nitin. Tavleen was not too happy at the developments and was a bit confused knowing that Nitin always made sure he talked to her directly about such arrangements and not leave it to someone else to inform her.

Just then suddenly Nitin Hazrara showed himself to Tavleen discretely making a hand gesture asking her to come over. Surprised and out of breath with the sudden appearance of her husband who was supposed to be on their yacht, Tavleen and the kids rushed over. Hazrara quickly got them into His station wagon. He started driving away without wasting any time heading for Yarmouth. Tavleen and the children expressed surprise and happiness at the same time when Nitin narrated the story of how he was cheated and captured and ultimately saved by an invisible force.

"Don't be naïve. You are under threat from a major group of thugs. My grand master and I are in our invisible form. An associate of ours managed to save you just in time. They, our opposition, are a well organized group of thugs called cleansers and they have been given instructions to kill all of you." said an invisible voice shocking Tavleen and the kids. The next Moment two persons materialized in the rear seats of the station wagon.

"We thank you most humbly for having saved our lives" said Hazrara.

"How is it possible for men to become invisible?" asked Shankar.

"May be they are Nava-Sadhus" said Shreya. "Where did you learn about the Nava-Sadhus" asked the younger one. Tavleen told him about the manuscript of Douglas Hilton. Hazrara was the most surprised. "Was anything mentioned about a struggle yet to happen""Yes indeed. We have no idea as to what it is, but" "What is now happening is no more than a part of the scheme of things that is valid. You will come to know many such things in due course. You should know that one of you is empowered to enter the fourth dimension" so saying he put his hand on Nitin and suddenly a glow came on the face of Nitin and involuntarily he started chanting a mantra to the utter consternation of the Hazrara family. "What is interesting to know is that Mr. Hazrara sitting here is an empowered human which he is not aware of" "How can this be? I have no knowledge of any thing that you have been talking about." said Nitin.

"Exactly. You will know more as we go along"

"Now about Shreya's comment that we may be Nava sadhus. She is not wrong. We are of a similar type serving mankind maintaining peace and increasing harmony. The real fun starts now. We will have to show the opposition a thing or two. You can help us Mr. Hazrara. However we are not out of danger yet. The evil ones will try to strike at any time and they have a huge network and enough destructive potential" said the elder one who looked like an ascetic with European features.

"I place myself, my wife Tavleen, my son Shankar and daughter Shreya as also my large network of offices, hotels and shops at your service without any reservation" said Nitin.

The other person, a handsome Youngman Alberto Rimini turned to Tavleen saying "Madam, you can help set the ball rolling. This is what we have in mind—"an interesting plan was sketched out.

"OK let's have fun and show the opposition their place" said Tavleen getting into the spirit of the moment.

The station wagon was cruising along merrily and the travelers were all in good spirits laughing and joking. As the vehicle approached Yarmouth, there was a colossal crash. A huge truck ran in at top speed impacting heavily on to the station wagon literally smashing it into pulp.

CHAPTER 20

Stalingrad

Carlos was back viewing the activity in the cleanser camp again thanks to the Arrow's inputs.

"I want you to get off your asses and start moving. We have an important assignment that I will tell you about, in a minute. I want those blooming spiritualist nincompoops done in once and for all. We have to take immediate action not only here but in other countries as well. Do you understand?" yelled Groznyy Malankayev, a trusted deputy of Nikolai Dimitriev addressing a group of several tough looking guys facing him in the executive conference room of the public relations division of the 'Moskva Gereskaya' in Stalingrad. There have been several concerted attacks on persons of Asian origin in Russia after scores of Russians had become members of a spiritual sect and had been initiated into meditation and other practices considered rebellious and anti-establishment. "I have successfully liquidated one of their so called masters on Friday and hope to add more to the list soon" "Don't boast about it so much Vassily. We all know how we lost three of our best commandos in the bargain due to your foolishness. You were too scared to accompany them to the camp organized by those foreigners who call it a shibir. You stayed back like a coward and had not cautioned our men on the risks involved."

"How in hell could anyone ever imagine the fellows to be so deadly in combat? Our men didn't take guns since there was checking at the gate."

"How many times have I told you to take no chances? You should've known from those in China where in earlier times the Buddhist monks developed deadly martial arts at Shaolin temple for protection. Anyway it's a long time ago. Be careful and take no chances. Now I want all of you to listen carefully. We have information that their so called great master living in London has set his experts worldwide to take on our bosses. We have been told to fly our men to London, Glasgow, New Jersey, Istanbul and Geneva to counter some of them. All other areas including English midlands are already covered by our associates who'll tear the blighters to bits. Let me now give you the details"

Malankayev rattled off the names and assignments and the flight arrangements and the contact details.

"Any questions? Go on ask me before this session is closed"

"I have one. These so called masters I find are ordinary looking fellows. They are from many ethnic backgrounds. How do we identify them and what powers do they have to counter us?"

"I am not going to waste my time lecturing about them. We go by the information given by our field operators. Your job is to confront and eliminate them at locations identified by our operators. Each of you has access to our operators in the area assigned. Any more questions?" There were none. Malankayev left the group and walked briskly to his special sedan fitted with many security features. The rest of them were getting ready to leave and were collecting their belongings and special kits.

"I have a question" said someone and Malankayev turned round maliciously and was ready to explode blurting out "Why didn't you ask me there?" and suddenly realized that the person asking the question was not a part of his team. "Who are you and who let you in here?"

"No one let me in. I came myself. I came to warn you to change your ways. Don't mess with the spiritual people"

"Get lost. You have breached security and are unfit to live." Malankayev drew his pistol and fired at the stranger who was well built handsome and smiling"

To Malankayev utter shock the bullet just dropped out of the pistol's barrel right there without traveling to its target.

"Your gun holds no scare for me. I can kill you this minute if I want to. It is not our policy to kill or harm any one whatever the provocation. We have our powers but rarely use them. There's still time for your cleanser goons to stop their pogrom" the stranger said and disappeared.

Malankayev realized for the first time that the spiritualists were people with superhuman powers. This realization scared him.

CHAPTER 21

London

Carlos through the Arrow saw the happenings in London and the media's attention on the fate of the Hazrara family.

"Mystery surrounds the Yacht Solaris".

"Four dead bodies found floating at sea in the Isle of Wight" said the 'Manchester Guardian. Similar headlines appeared in the Times of London and other newspapers including the Telegraph and the Sun.

'News of the World" splashed gory details of the discovery.

Reports in the press suggested that the bodies were of Asians, perhaps a family, a husband, a wife a son and a daughter. There was also a story doing the rounds that it could be the family of Nitin Hazrara, a London businessman of Indian origin who owned a hotel chain and other companies apart from the luxury Yacht Solaris lying all decked up in the waters of the Isle of Wight.

The police however were tight lipped saying that the bodies were in a decomposed state making identification difficult. There were no personal papers, or other means of identification on any of the bodies making it difficult for the police to proceed with their investigation. The Hazrara family had gone missing from their London mansion while on their way to the Isle of Wight. Their Chauffer and their car were missing as well. Scotland Yard found no trace of any one including the chauffer or the car or the four members of the Hazrara family despite hectic efforts.

Suddenly the media caught on to the story. "Indian family murdered and bodies thrown into the sea" screamed banner headlines giving information of the tragedy of the multi millionaire that owned the yacht

Solaris. There was a write up on the financial stature of the missing Indian family's considerable business ventures, of the palatial house, their Hotel chain, retail outlets, their luxurious yacht and the farm house. Particulars of the family owned car and its chauffer both of them missing and untraced as yet by the London police were highlighted. All this, was put out by the press and the visual media, making the police look ineffective. Under pressure and in order to baulk the media the police released a press note saying 'Two business associates working for the Hazrara group of companies have been formally taken into custody for interrogation. No charges have been filed against them as yet, pending further investigation."

The police renewed their efforts to trace the Hazrara car and its driver. It was established that the car was on the highway from Kensington to Clapham but was seen no more after that. Enquiry at the Southampton ferry point revealed that the car had not been on any ferry to East Cowes in the Isle of Wight.

At the Isle of Wight the bodies recovered from the sea around the yacht Solaris were sent for postmortem examination. The cause of death could not be clearly established as due to drowning. The identity could not be established of any of the bodies due to their decomposed state.

CHAPTER 22

London

Guided by the Arrow Carlos saw how the life of a young Indian businessman changed after he traveled to London and Nairobi.

"I'm off to London tonight Mom"

"For how long?"

"It depends, could be a week or a couple more. I've to tie up with a contact"

"Is the contact a female?"

"Yes, but don't jump to conclusions"

"How old is she and what does she do?"

"She's around twenty five and owns a mining company in Africa. She wants me to help her obtain mining leases in Kenya"

"Be careful and return soon. I haven't forgotten your last escapade with that Spanish female"

"That was a disaster mom. It's not going to be repeated"

"I'm not sure. You come back soon and that's it"

"Will do" said Pramod Shingaraya.

His mom Gayatri was the chairperson of the Shingaraya group based in Goa and Bangalore, India, controlling several multinational companies. Pramod was an only son born after many years of prayer and visits to holy places.

Her husband Suresh now lived like a recluse. He went away to Rishikesh in North India joining an Ashram on turning sixty—five. He left home giving up all corporate activity saying he had enough of the rat race and wanted peace above all else.

Pramod landed at Heathrow Airport and drove to India House in Aldwych in a luxury sedan hired from a car rental agency. He met up with an Indian Embassy official Mr. Mitra and obtained a letter of introduction to the Kenyan Government's minister of Industry copied to the Indian Ambassador in Kenya.

"Be careful while dealing with the Kenyan Government. They are sticklers to rules and go by the book. Any deviation will be counter productive" advised Mr. Mitra trade secretary at the Indian Embassy.

Promod headed for Adam Street in the Strand area to meet up with his friend Miss. Cynthia, daughter of the industrial tycoon Sir Richard Harlow of South Africa who had an office in London.

Cynthia was waiting for Pramod. After the initial greetings Cynthia broached the subject of her interest.

"I've looked up the mining scenario in Kenya and Uganda. The natural soda ash mining I feel may be profitable. I want you to go to Kenya and try to obtain long term leases"

"How about Fluorspar, Diatomite and limestone?"

"We could also look at these perhaps later, after we set foot there" said Cynthia

"I need to spend a few days here in London"

"Please do. I intend going with you to Nairobi and Mombassa"

"That'll make things easier"

Pramod drove down to his St. James Palace hotel. He went around visiting his old haunts in London for the next three days.

On the fourth day he felt somewhat tired and went to sleep. He dreamt of his younger days of delightful bonding with his father, their frequent trips to exotic places in India and abroad. The whole thing was like a motion picture and suddenly it stopped. Pramod woke up and felt confused. His watch showed thetime. It was four in the morning. For a second he wasn't sure where he was. He switched on the TV and surfed around. He switched off and tried to sleep. He fell into a fitful sleep. Once again the motion picture started in his dream. This time a bearded person appeared and talked. "Get ready now to play a part that appears mysterious. You will take on another person's memory bank preserving your own. This will happen in Kenya. You will meet a person called Odumba Kylele. Just follow whatever he says"

The dream TV screen went dark but lighted up again giving the same message. This pattern started happening continuously. Pramod awoke and found he was sweating. The phone rang

"Hey it's Cynthia here" Pramod heard on his phone.

"I'm real glad you called"

"Why? Is anything wrong?

"No. Just that I have had very little sleep and a fitful one at that"

"I'm sorry. I phoned to tell you that I made all arrangements for our stay in Nairobi and Mombassa. You have to choose the day of travel as my agents have blocked two first class seats for all of next week for London-Nairobi flights on the British Airways"

"Done. I've decided to leave sooner. I need to buy a few things which I'll do today"

'May be we'll have dinner at the little Armenian Restaurant in Soho you're so fond of"

"O.K. Let's meet there at around seven"

"Suits me. I've some material from the Minerals year book released in advance on the mining statistics for Kenya. I'll give it to you to study"

"Meet you at seven then"

Pramod took a shower had scrambled eggs on toast and coffee. He left the hotel at ten thirty.

He visited Regent Street for some shopping and returned to the hotel for lunch. When he picked his room key at the reception there was a message from someone called George Lloyd. "Please give me a call when you get back. I would like to meet with you for a few minutes. I am from Nairobi, Kenya" a telephone number was mentioned in the note.

Pramod was surprised that someone from Kenya wanted to meet him but was not keen to call back. He went on the computer and started reading about the Nairobi National Park close to the city of Nairobi in Kenya. It was close to five when he finished.

Pramod was an outdoor man and hated to stay confined inside the house or hotel room or wherever else he stayed. Apart from working out to keep fit, he liked running. Participation in Marathons of various cities held from time to time had seen his enthusiastic participation. He once traveled all the way to Paris from Goa just for such an event.

He now saw he had a couple of hours to spare before meeting Cynthia that evening. He headed for the in—house gym at the hotel. As he was trying to step out of his room, the phone rang. It was from the reception informing him that a Mr. Lloyd was waiting in the lounge to see him. Promod went down to the reception and had the girl there call Mr. Lloyd to come over and meet him. Mr. Lloyd was a tall burly bearded man of non African origin which came as a bit of a surprise since Pramod was expecting a Kenyan.

"I am Pramod Shingaraya"

"I know. Good Afternoon. I have friends in India who have given me your hotel number here in London with other details"

Mr. Lloyd then went on "I have through a certain mental process come to know of the strange dream that is troubling you. The dream is meant to prepare you for a purpose of great importance to the world. I'll meet you in Nairobi and take you to this man called Odumba Kylele. He is close to a hundred years in age."

Pramod was stunned.

"For God's sake, why me of all people for this experiment?"

"You are right. It's for God's sake indeed"

"Miss Cynthia Harlow travels with me to Nairobi"

"I know that. You will finish her work of obtaining mining leases. She'll afterwards actively help you in your mission"

"How do you say that?"

"She will be contacted and informed of the importance of your mission. Your mother has also been informed and has given her consent"

'All this sounds pretty strange to me. I am not highly educated and had wasted my early youth in the pursuit of pleasure rather than anything useful"

"Your 'incarnation—history' is great. You were in a previous birth, a great thinker and activist called Rousseau of French descent"

"This is incredible"

Things moved pretty fast thereafter. Pramod and Cynthia reached Nairobi and attended to the task at hand of obtaining mining leases from the Kenyan Government. Mr. Lloyd met up with Pramod and took him to Odumba Kylele. In a session lasting over an hour, while Pramod sat quietly, Odumba Kylele who was an aide to the biblical king Solomon in one of his past lives transferred his memory bank by bulk-mind mail to Pramod who received it in tact. "I have two memory banks now, what do I do?" asked Pramod.

"That's the beauty. You can use any one of them at any time by switching it on. The other remains passive. This is the secret of many spiritual masters and grand masters. They even have the power to access the memory bank of others temporarily when they come face to face. You should be glad of your power" Said Lloyd.

CHAPTER 23

Singapore

Carlos guided by the Arrow continued to view the Indian businessman Pramod's life and action. The arrow said that one shouldn't be surprised seeing the arrow in the scenario at times

Lloyd renamed Pramod as Rousseau Hitha and sent him to Singapore where Pramod attained astral travel and other spiritual powers to become a spiritual master. He was groomed by a Russian grand master who remained in constant touch.

Rousseau Hitha started his discourses on a regular basis in Singapore at different locations to members of Kosmica and others.

One day a huge gathering of men and women sat in pin drop silence, eager to listen to this spiritual master Rousseau Hitha who held them spell-bound every time he spoke.

"Any discussion on spirituality has to take off from a point that shows that it is some thing that is capable of being felt or experienced. For a start it could be a traditional belief about inner space named 'the kingdom of God' that is within us as declared by Jesus. If you have faith in Jesus you will naturally consider this to be true and all further action to explore that kingdom becomes easy as you have no doubt about its presence within you. It does not matter to you whether this inner space is there or not in other humans or in non-human species inhabiting our world."

"What about God and our concept of him or her?" asked Alberto Rimini a member in the audience. The master started speaking of God:

"Another traditional concept is about God. Not being given the power to distinguish between a hallucination and a so called divine spiritual experience, one is forced to fall back on the concept of God which is a faith oriented issue rather than an intellect-logic oriented one. For example Jesus Christ said he was the son and that his father had sent him and that the kingdom of God is within us. We thus have three concepts namely of 'God depicted as the father', 'his kingdom within us' and 'his Son sent to us in the human form'. All these are based on faith. Taking the first two concerning God, several humans revered as prophets or Avatars have spoken of him or her. Scriptures of most religions have asserted God's status as the creator of the universe as also the one who is full of unconditional love and most forgiving but rather a strict and punishing father-mother figure. Perhaps the Buddhist lore is the only one that does not define God and has no concept of such a phenomenon. Some of the subtler religions declare God to be the un-seeable, un-understandable, un-definable, omnipotent, all pervading entity with no beginning middle or end, ever present in the smallest of the small and the biggest of the big and so on.""Don't you think that it is a correct attitude for such exploration of God's power?" asked someone. "Our exploration concerning spiritual phenomena is flawed since we are forced to accept the existence of something or some one called God with no proof and no structured logic at least as understood by our mind stuff to be able to proceed further in the matter."

"Who created the universe is a question begging some reply" said Alberto Rimini.

"Yes. I agree. One major belief system does not mention the creation of the universe and does not attribute it to the one that it considers to be the 'Supreme Being'. It only mentions the Supreme Being as the dispenser of justice by way of reward or punishment that too after death. In other words the belief system only concerns itself with dispensing of justice and administration of all that is already in existence and is non committal about how or who created it or when"

The master stopped his interactive session as something else apparently gained his attention, perhaps a telepathic message. The master left after saying "I'm sorry my dear friends. I have to leave now. I will be back in a short while and resume the session. Meanwhile I suggest you do meditation and chanting"

The master got into his astral travel sheath for a meeting in an icy cave in the southern Himalayan range. The master's Guru a person of Russian origin known as 'Ishatma' was already there and the two, submerged in blissful love and mutual respect, conversed directly through their soundless frequency medium." Master there is urgent need for you to know certain things. Our empowered mantra master who was working to identify certain negative persons on this planet and their modus operandi is under threat of elimination. There is a comprehensive security cell in the fourth dimension known to you. The guard ensemble there has discovered a joint collaboration of several wealthy billionaires; all arms manufacturers on the planet Earth. It is to subvert the spiritual centers radiating waves of 'peace-inducing' vibrations to counter the harmful effects of human conflict engineered by powerful negative forces."

"Are these guards not empowered to deal with such a situation effectively, grand master?"

"Well, you are correct in part, but there are many aspects that come into the picture. I will now put you wise to the whole system of controls since you may also be required to take certain actions from time to time."

"I'll be ever ready Grand master to do my bit"

"Beings on the earth comprising close to six billion humans apart from billions and billions of other species are always in danger of a man made catastrophe. Man is the only creature in this planet that has the potential to destroy every thing by his actions. Man's six vices namely lust, anger, miserliness, greed, arrogance and jealousy as you know are a part of his baser nature and lead to unpredictable actions jeopardizing the planet's normal vibration—balance. The Sacred awareness therefore has put a system in place to negate this possibility. You have now been selected to join the system and are assigned to the Asia region." How does one qualify and how many are there, grand master?"

"There are fifteen regions covering the planet's surface. Each region has ten super conscious beings like you called Mahans that have the facility of third realm access. I have called you to tell you that you as a Mahan are now with us"

"How was I selected? What is my ultimate role, kindly enlighten me"

"You already know about the unique type of instantaneous vertical vibration which has a different scale of frequencies unlike any other vibration in space. The Mahans create and maintain higher and positive waves of frequency by their power of concentrated thought vibration to avert harm. Mahans may be in any part of the planet but are responsible for their regions. The Sacred awareness gives the third realm access capability to individuals selected purely on incarnate merit. The individuals thus selected may not be conforming to the norms of worldly worthiness such as high erudition or royal birth and so on but are chosen solely on merit, of past incarnations. Out of these individuals some are chosen as Mahans. You, master, were selected likewise."

"How wonderful indeed that I am selected although in the present incarnation I was only a businessman with no high education."

"You, master, have surpassed many of your peers in your mastery of astral abilities."

"Respects Grand master, May I know how you came to be a part of this?"

"Placed in the role of a coordinator I am a Mahatho. There are two Mahathos like me for each region to constantly monitor the status from the Mahans of the region. A Mahatho is normally one that has acted as a Guru to third realm access empowered individuals. I am in your region and we will work together from now on. We have to counter the cleansers."

"Who are the so called cleansers and how do they act?"

"The cleansers group is a powerful organization of many committed men and women. It is an army; navy and air force all rolled into one, a syndicate with active presence in almost all countries.

"Who set it up?"

"The syndicate has been put together by a group of powerful and influential super rich persons connected with armament manufacture worth billions and billions of American dollars. They are convinced that spiritual persons are a threat to normal humans who are driven by a market economy.

"How can they say so?"

"By introducing new and strange ideas the spiritual men and women in their opinion undermine the fabric of human society. The cleansers feel that redemption of sinners through the medium of the various well defined religious orders is essential for people to remain committed to one religion or the other helping to perpetuate a mind set of conflict and assertion of might through wars."

"Even so how does spiritualism become a threat to these people?"

"They are worried about the doctrine of reincarnation which is considered dangerous and confusing. They are afraid that the manufacture and sale of arms and military equipment that needs human conflicts is at great risk of obliteration".

"I understand. Unless they ensure a never ending human conflict and war, this industry that rakes in huge profits will collapse."

"Yes. There is enormous political support for them from the hawks of all nations. They intend to kill or destroy all those who are trying to spread peace and harmony and trying to save the world from conflict through spiritual means."

"How does the Upper Dimension set up go about to counter the cleansers?"

"The UD set up is unique and multi faceted. It is bound by a code of conduct that prohibits direct action from their dimension against those in the third dimension that includes the earth.

"What about entry into its domain?" They in UD ensure that no one from the third dimension who is not specially empowered has access to it. The only exception is the special empowerment given to the spiritual grand masters who do not have to seek permission."

"Is there no other exception?"

"Yes there is. Four 'non—spiritual' persons who have special merit based on their incarnation record are permitted to enter. They are permitted only once. These empowered ones will only come to know about their special power at the time of action as decided by the UD guards. It is where one of the two judgment centers is located to deal with the astral bodies of those who leave the third dimension at the time of ending their incarnation, the so called 'death'"

"Are there any other planets with living beings?"

"Earth is only one of a few planets in the universe with life forms"

"I believe that only the life forms of the moving kind with limbs have astral bodies and not the non-moving or non-limbed ones on earth."

"You are right. The so called non moving ones including matter with its components of atoms and subatomic particles as also the non-limbed life forms such as insects and other smaller 'life-forms' including bacteria die and reincarnate in the same third dimension through a transformation process native to it."

"Is it then our duty as human-beings or entities capable of moving in the fourth or other dimensions to act to counter the cleansers?"

"Yes. The sacred awareness always acts through the intelligent beings in the third dimension. That is why we have this program of negating the harmful vibrations apart from dealing with the cleansers directly once we know them. We are to physically interact using our powers if necessary to thwart their evil design."

"I am with you grandmaster all the way. Please accept my respects."

"I convey my Respects to you indeed, master" said the grandmaster.

The meeting in the cave came to an end.

CHAPTER 24

Singapore

Carlos saw a demonstration of the powers of spiritual masters with clarity thanks to the Arrow.

Rousso Hitha returned to his audience and resumed his discourse.

"I will today give you the benefit of witnessing a profound truth. Meanwhile ask me any question to clear your doubts."

"We have the word of many exalted personages describing their interaction with God. Do you consider them to be valid proof of God's existence?" asked a member of the audience.

"Our Himalayan seers declare that one can experience God when one's ego is obliterated leading to a merger of one's self with the universal self which may perhaps be called God, the individual self becoming a sub-part of that God. There is also the primary concept of peace, happiness, joy or bliss one is capable of experiencing in stages of greater and greater intensity by a process of a dedicated effort that includes meditation and chanting among other things. Mention is also made of energy infusion techniques that activate certain nodal centers of the human body leading to transcendental experiences of bliss"

"How far these are authentic and not merely the result of a rearrangement of the brain's chemical composition?" asked someone.

"Yes, it is a point to ponder. The need to establish the fact that no external chemical substance is taken into the body to produce such a feeling of bliss becomes important and the inducement of a chemical reaction in one's mind purely by an action of one's mind, intellect or the vibration generated by elements of one's own body, border on the bizarre or the miraculous,' said the master.

"What about those god-men who though illiterate and uneducated had risen to the very pinnacle of spiritual greatness without ever studying the scriptures or philosophy?" asked another member from the congregation?

"It is a very valid question. Man is only said to be discovering whatever there already is and knowledge is one of the things that already exists and can be tapped into by anyone who through his mind attains a state of receptivity. It then becomes a matter of switching the brain to the right frequency that could be done either by meditation or by some other technique. These great men perhaps know an alternate way of switching." The master said.

Suddenly there was a commotion and some members of the audience got up and started moving towards an approaching woman dressed in yellow robes. Apparently she was someone known and respected by many. The master smiled at the woman.

Pointing to a chair next to him, he said "Sister Uma, May I request you to please join me here" It will be an honor far beyond what I deserve" said the woman and walked towards the master." Please listen carefully" said the master addressing the audience after the woman sat on the chair. "Sister Uma being herself a master is a person that has attained a position in the realm of spirituality that you may call mind blowing" he continued speaking,

"The scientists tell us that we humans normally use only a very little portion of our brain. That is correct. The other parts come into play when we enter the finer sheaths "said the master.

The master then turned towards Uma and said "Please explain to them the meaning of de-materialization of the five—sheathed human body"

Uma got up and started addressing the gathering

"I am indeed grateful to the master for his kind words of introduction. I owe my spiritual progress to the master's kind guidance and instruction. Let me now give you an over-view of what the human body comprises of. One's gross body sheathed in skin is the basic gross form with a given name that one normally identifies with his or her personality. The fact is that this gross body is called the 'food nurtured' sheath. There are four other finer and subtler sheaths that shroud the body which are called 'The mind nurtured sheath' 'the life nurtured sheath' 'the knowledge nurtured sheath' and finally 'the joy or bliss nurtured sheath'. Sometimes two or three of the sheaths are considered as one sheath namely those of the mind, life and knowledge, thus reducing the sheaths to three. These are not visible to the human eye. Yoga teaches us the way to access these sheaths to transport one to wherever one wishes in one of these sheaths. Each sheath has a corresponding mind stuff that comes into play as we access the sheaths."

"How does the mind function as one goes into meditation? Does one experience each of these minds associated with the five sheaths one after the other?" asked Alberto Rimini a person from the audience.

"Yes indeed. That is the purpose of their presence. As one progresses away from the first mind stuff associated with the gross body, the other minds take over at each stage and the final stage is bliss or Amanda. A person returns to the gross mind when the bliss stage is consciously ended" said Uma replying to the query.

Suddenly the place became hazy and Uma disappeared. The master said "Let us prepare our minds to accept a fact that defies 'Physical laws' as we understand them. Uma wanted to show and give us the answer as to how it is possible for one to de-materialize one's body stuff to disappear from view. Uma is very much here but in a different dimension from the dimension in which we exist. She cannot communicate with any of us except through the mind. She has the power however to create whatever she wishes in our dimension before materializing herself back to be with us."

The silence that greeted this statement was total. The audience was in a state of shock and disbelief.

The next moment Uma reappeared and started speaking. "I know how unreal all this will look to most of you. The master is yet to reveal some other important detail about my disappearance. I now request him to speak to us about it."

The master spoke "Uma is right. There are various ways in which true yogis can act if they wish to. Physical disappearance is the first and basic act of leaving our dimension as demonstrated by sister Uma. A yogi who attains the power called 'swa-drisya' can stay in his body while at the same time manifest himself in any manner or form in a place of his choice using one of the sheaths other than his food nurtured sheath namely his body. He can then be in more than one place temporarily at any given time."

A long and interesting session of questions and answers followed. The master explained many of the concepts concerning the world as it exists for us the humanoids. When someone asked a question about the food the master gave an illuminating discourse.

The word 'Food' while it rings a bell does not however transport one into an intellectual or analytical frame of mind.

At most the word instantly appeals to one's sense of taste as also to one's basic hunger fulfillment and perhaps in due course reminds one of items like meat, bread, fish, milk, cereal, fruit etc. that are essential ingredients in the preparation of one's breakfast lunch dinner supper etc. which have to be eaten regularly to ensure that one continues to live each day. We have the famous prayer in the Bible asking the almighty to give us our daily bread among other things.

It is surprising but true that our ancestors in India had thoroughly examined what food meant in real terms. They called it '*Annam*'. They said "*Annamayam Jagat*' (The world consists of food).

They also came up with certain commandments as to the do's and the don'ts regarding food.

Three of these commandments are as follows;

- ✓ *Annam Na Nindyaat Tad Vratam. (As a sacred commitment thou shall not abuse food)*
- ✓ *Annam Na Parichacsheeta Tad Vratam (As a sacred commitment thou shall not detest food)*
- ✓ *Annam Bahu Kurveeta Tad Vratam (As a sacred commitment thou shall multiply food)*

An interesting explanation follows each of the above commandments to say that 'Life is based on food and the body is sustained by food. Life is dependent on the body and the body is dependent on life. Therefore food is based on food and whoever realizes this will never lack it and will be prosperous in all respects and will be shining with knowledge etc . . . . '.

Further examples of a) fire and water their nature and their interdependence on food and b) Earth (matter) and sky (space) their nature and interdependence on food are cited.

What does all this mean? Is it the ranting of an incoherent mind wanting to confuse one and all? ; Certainly not. It stands as a shining beacon of intuitive knowledge of the highest degree the human mind can comprehend. All creatures in this world have to eat one another to live. In other words living beings eat other living beings to prolong life. Trees and plants have been proven to be living and are not exempt from this chain of living beings. Man the undisputed lord as he seems to think himself to be, is also food to a wild beast or to other cannibals. So the entire world is sustained by food. Life (food) cannot exist without other life (food).

Food has to be fresh to sustain life. Man has resorted to refrigeration of slaughtered animals and uprooted and lifeless vegetables and calls it a technique of preservation invented by him. Man forgets that God or whoever is the one who designed our order of things was a million times cleverer. A structure with myriad components such as vital organs and miles of nerves and arteries circulating blood and systems for oxygenation and elimination of wastes and glands and all else in a complex self programmed growth and decline is inbuilt in all living creatures keeping them ever fresh to be killed and eaten by other creatures to keep the world eternally running in its cycle. Each creature is maintained at its optimum temperature fresh and ready as food and not as dead carcasses inadequately refrigerated in manmade machines to be preserved as food fit for eating.

The last dictum of multiplying food is attained by procreation of the species apart from other modes such as raising crops by man.

CHAPTER 25

London

The Arrow transported Carlos back to Hazrara's affairs and the narration continued.

There was a notification that went out to the employees of all companies of the Hazrara group.

'We are aware that each one of you is sad at the strange disappearance and the failure of attempts by the police to trace Mr. Hazrara his wife and two children. The police are now investigating the identity of four bodies found floating in the waters of the Isle of Wight which we pray and hope are not those of our chairman Mr. Nitin Hazrara and his family members.

Pending the results of police investigation and their further action, we the undersigned have taken control of all companies owned by

Hazrara Holdings Limited and will be issuing directives from time to time for their proper running for mandatory implementation by the chief executives of the companies. We have initiated our own extensive investigation to get at the truth concerning the disappearance of the Hazrara family.

For and on behalf of Hazrara Holdings Limited

We the trustees affix our signatures below along with the company seal on this day as noted in London

    Hardy Singh   Margie Boyd   Avinash Behara
                (Trustee directors)

Immediate instructions went out to the chief executives of all Hazrara group companies notifying the appointment of the firm 'Lall & Murty' as authorized investigators and directing that all assistance be rendered to representatives of the firm to progress their work. A separate account of expenses was to be maintained in that respect.

The three trustee directors represent the Hazrara trust as its nominees in the holding company that owned the group. The other directors of the holding company are Hazrara himself, Tavleen and Mr. Brewster.

M/s Lall & Murty the 'law and support services' providing firm headquartered in Nairobi, Kenya had branches in London, Liverpool and Edinburgh. The firm has been close to the Hazrara group. Mr. Nitin Hazrara's father had regular contacts with the firm and had known the partners well.

Singh, Boyd and Behara were close friends of the senior Hazrara. He inducted them into the trust.

After the demise of his father, Nitin maintained status-quo and the arrangement was running well. Hardev (Hardy) Singh was chairman of his own family bank 'Hingh Bank'. Margie (short for Margaret) Boyd was managing partner of the famous law firm 'Ray, Boyd & Chester' and Avinash was running a management consulting company called 'Clear Eye Services' that had a roaring business in Kenya, the United Kingdom and Mauritius.

Lall & Murty assigned Jay Mithra and Bob Williams to carry out a special investigation from their London office into all aspects relating to Hazrara disappearance giving them a free hand with no bar on expenses.

Jay Mithra, a strapping six foot two in his socks had seen it all. Murders and mayhem, petty crime, fraud, cheating or whatever, nothing floored him. He had a high eighty percent success rate in bringing culprits to justice. An army man originally, Mithra branched off into corporate administration and management heading a division of a multi national company in Canada. Somehow feeling a bit lost he took up journalism becoming a reporter for a reputed Newspaper covering petty crime and murder.

"Jay, why don't you become a detective on a full time basis? Think about it and let me know if you want to." said Editor Watson when Mithra had gone to him one day to file a report on an intricate case of murder.

Mithra's response was immediate.

"Jim, I am game if you have a job for me."

The next thing, Jay Mithra became a partner in charge of the detective division of 'Lall & Murty', posted in their London office. He plunged into his job headlong and very soon the results started showing. His journalist career and army experience helped.

Bob Williams an agile and well built man was a regular detective having served with Scotland Yard for a number of years. He was an expert martial arts man with black belts in karate and tai-Kwan-do. He was brought into the company by Mithra.

The break-through came when the detective duo of Mithra and Williams happened to trace a call received by Hazrara on the thirteenth June at ten past noon from the Embassy of Suleimania in London, which the Scotland Yard had earlier noted but had considered it as unimportant knowing Hazrara to be a businessman with many interests including official dealings with the Embassies of various countries and that such phone calls were routine.

'We were checking out if there were any phone calls from private individuals or organizations." The police said.

Mithra and Williams called on the Embassy and after some painstaking exercise of prodding were able to establish the vital link.

It was Sayed Karimi of the embassy that had made a phone call to Hazrara on 13th June. Karimi's interrogation led to the fact that a team from Schwarz & Associates was sent to the family house of Nitin Hazrara.

"May we have a word with these guys called Schwarz & Associates that had met Mr. Hazrara at his home, please?"

Williams asked Karimi.

Karimi was at the phone for a while after which he turned to Mithra and said

"As a matter of fact it's a long story. There was a message to us from M/s Miller Smith Holdings who are the authorized executors of several huge projects in Suleimania worth billions of pounds. They wanted us to contact Mr. Hazrara and convey to him that he is selected to execute the hotel project under advice from the President of Suleimania.

Mr. Schwarz and the others were sent by Miller Smith Holding. Mr. Hazrara had called our Ambassador who spoke with him. We have had no other contact"

"Will it be possible for you to phone Miller Smith Holdings and get them to give us the contact numbers of Schwarz & Associates?"

"Sure, why not? I'll do it right now" Karimi phoned the Miller outfit and spoke with them and replied

"Sorry. They say they organized the whole thing at the request of the foreign office of Suleimania and the team of Mr. Schwarz is not working for them anymore and they have no address or phone number of Mr. Schwarz."

"Why not ask your people in Suleimania?"

"We asked our ministry in Suleimania. They said that the infrastructure related contract in the Islamic Republic of Suleimania worth around two billion dollars was a genuine one that required the selected contracting company to travel to Zavros to sign the contract with the representatives of the consultants authorized by the president of Suleimania."

"Alright, could you check with them if the contract has been signed at Zavros by Mr. Hazrara?"

Karimi spoke to his people. "Yes. Mr. Hazrara has signed. Mr. Hazrara has not visited Suleimania yet but the project work has started there".

Bob Williams set to work and unearthed the people that owned the corporate giant Miller-smith Holdings. All relevant information was immediately passed on to M/s Lall & Murty.

Lall immediately got Mr. Bainbridge on a long distance call and conveyed the information and outlined the proposed course of action he had in mind;

"I've some vital info that our detectives unearthed. Mr. Hazrara has signed a huge project in Suleimania. A company which has control over the project has sent its men to contact him at his house on the fateful day of the family's disappearance. He then traveled to a place in Uruguay to sign the contract worth two billion pounds sterling. There is some mischief that this company is perhaps trying to cover up. It will be in our interest to investigate the company's background more thoroughly using utmost caution. We have the list of persons that own the corporate house of Miller—smith that was involved. They are members of the Board and shareholders as well. Sixty percent of the shares are held by them while the rest is widely dispersed. The names are

Oscar Miller, James Warner, Nikolai Dimitriev, Julio Fernandez, Adamji Amanathulla, Joseph Bartholomew, John Balasingham, Bill Mackenzie, Reza Tabsili and Mark Hoffman.

We have prepared dossiers on each of them from available information. We are also preparing notes on those of their associate companies having questionable activities. We do not propose to investigate the holding company directly which may turn out to be counterproductive."

"Please have the notes and dossiers sent by special messenger to me right away. Thanks for the effort and congrats for the break-through. I'll be in touch. Also please keep the indirect investigations going "said Bainbridge a personal confidant of Parama who is called the great master. Bainbridge consulted the great master when the list arrived.

"Take action to save the world I would say. Murder and Mayhem is not for us. You may deal with these cleansers in a manner that would deprive them of their money power making them give up their evil ways. You may avail of the Hazrara millions placed at our disposal for this good cause" Said the master.

"What about the project in Suleimania?"

"That one will not suffer. It has already commenced has it not? The absence on the spot of Nitin Hazrara apparently is not to matter."

"Yes, great Master. We'll progress the counter-blow in the manner desired and pay all attention to the financial aspect"

"There may be bigger fish that are involved. Get full financial information of all companies and the nodal control criteria of assets in each case and formulate your action plan to de-nude them money-wise. I will request the other masters to assist you" said the great master. Bainbridge had one last question "Just in case, we encounter unprovoked violence from the other side, do we have your permission to retaliate? I need your guidance great master."

"Violence is evil and particularly so if it is unprovoked. Yet, you have the moral right to react using violence in the degree needed in each such case without any inhibition. But firstly always explore the avenues for transforming the evil men into men of peace"

Bainbridge departed fully satisfied.

Immediate steps were put in motion to deal with the situation. All committed and dedicated contact persons in the various stock exchanges and bourses world-wide were alerted and briefed about the action required in each case, in respect of the companies of the cleanser leaders.

Results started showing sooner than expected. By the third day there was a marked downward trend in the prices of shares of five of the companies owned by these leaders.

"Blimey who in bloody hell is playing around with my shares?" became a common refrain of the owners of the really big cleanser companies.

Fresh investigation gave the identity of three super powerful members of the so called "High Command "that controlled Miller-Smith and other outfits. These three top men were arms manufacturers of international stature well entrenched politically in most countries particularly with their defense outfits and ministries of finance and commerce. All three kept a low profile and were rarely seen or photographed. They always worked through their subordinates and had special teams to carry out strong-arm maneuvers including murder to promote their local and global interests.

There was a belief in the Cleanser camp that a grand master of the spiritual brigade was actually helping the cleanser cause. The identity of this mysterious person was a closely guarded secret and was never discussed in any meeting of the cleanser leaders.

CHAPTER 26

London

Carlos saw Bainbridge's life and times as shown by the Arrow.

Brian Bainbridge a man of deep conviction was born in the Bay area in California in the United States. After a stint as an assistant professor in the university guiding research in physics, he got interested in eastern philosophy and yoga. Within a span of five years he was on top in his spiritual progress earning respect from his peers and appreciation from his master. He attained third realm empowerment during meditation pleasing his master and guide immensely. This gave him the power to access higher dimensions such as the fourth and beyond. He never considered himself as some one special despite these powers. He was endowed with a muscular body and great stamina. Bainbridge was well versed in self defense being a great martial arts enthusiast.

Bainbridge was the invisible driver that saved Nitin Hazrara from his captors on the Isle of Wight. Once the Hazrara family got into the station wagon the task was taken over by one of the other masters ably assisted by his disciple a handsome young man named Alberto Rimini.

Carlos guided by the Arrow went back to view the spiritualists' special protection unit.

"This is Mason wanting a word with you. I've finalized your team"

"Go ahead. I'm ready and keen to brief them."

"Exactly that's what I want to talk about. I've prepared some reference documents which are on their way. Within the next ten minutes you'll receive dossiers with full details and photographs. The team is now all yours and will remain so. The members will individually report to you between four and five this afternoon and receive your instructions. They are presently put up in Hotel Horizon across Holborn on Russell Street. I suppose you'll want to shift them which is fine"

"I expect they will each one come to me separately showing no signs of mutual recognition even if they happen to see one another."

"Yes, that's how it'll happen"

"Fine"

Bainbridge received the dossiers as indicated and took a look at them. The first one was about Frederick Stoldt a German from Bremerhaven, 26 years of age having good features, a black belt in Kung-fu and a University degree in mathematics. The others had equally impressive pedigree. Thus Timothy graham, Sui Wu and Hilda Meyer passed muster with their respective dossiers.

All the four were closeted with Bainbridge.

"You are as of this moment a part of an army of commandos to fight the menace of a narrow and perverted group of highly paid mercenaries out to destroy all spiritual masters on earth and their followers irrespective of their religious background or spiritual stature. Each of you will undergo a series of intense initiation sessions during which an enlightened spiritual master will empower you with rare capabilities and skills that will help overcome all manners of opposition"

"Where is this to take place?" asked Frederick.

"Right here in London and one of the greatest will do the initiation. However you will be put through some assessment related routine for skill evaluation. Individual envelopes have been prepared for each of you with your names written on them. You will read the material placed in the envelopes and will follow the instructions given there. You will travel separately and shift to the places mentioned. You will interact with me on one to one basis. Tasks will be assigned to you and you are to carry them out with no questions asked. I now gladly welcome you into the team."

The team left Bainbridge and retired to their accommodation. Each of them had carried their envelops with them to be opened.

Frederick Stoldt opened the envelop Bainbridge had given him and read the contents.

"Frederick Please proceed to West Germany. Go first to Hamburg and then you may have to go to Bremen. Your tickets and money are in the folder. The job is very delicate involving collection of information about threats to our Max Centers on Baunhoff Strasse in Hamburg and next to the Rathausmarkt in Bremen. Contact a lady called Emma by phone (see number on slip stapled). You need not contact me before you leave London. Be in touch with me for planning your return travel after learning from Emma of the existing situation and threat perception at first hand. Emma will introduce you to the people in the center at Hamburg who in turn will provide you with all necessary assistance including accommodation and supply of cash for meeting your expenses."

Frederick traveled from London to Harwich and caught an overnight ferry to the Hoek van Holland and on reaching there caught a connecting train to Hamburg early in the morning. He had breakfast in the dining car. Having recently lived in London, he now saw how comparatively expensive food in Europe had become after the war. The train chugged on from Holland entering West Germany after the usual stop at the border station for checking of identity papers. Frederick got off at the Hauptbaunhof the central station in Hamburg. He came out on the northern exit gate and walked along the pavement wanting to locate the Max center of enlightenment that was named after Maxmuller the German spiritual leader who made a deep study of the world's spiritual literature as also the thought patterns of ancient people about heaven, hell and God.

He didn't have to go far. Within a hundred meters of the north gate of the station he could see the sign board of the spiritual center written in Deutsch the main language of the Germans. Hamburger Platt the low Deutsch language as against the Hock or the high one is popular in the city as Stoldt was well aware. He knew them both including some interesting literature in each.

The office of the Spiritual center was modest and functional with no frills. A young man was there to greet Frederic and spoke to him in Deutsch "I am Ralph. We were told about your visit. The office is run by a voluntary staff of three persons and normally is kept open from 9 in the morning till 5.30 in the evening. I specially came today to receive you. Please feel free to use our service." Frederick was happy. He phoned Emma and came to know of the arrangements made for his stay and the transport details. She asked him to proceed to his guest room in the home of a Yoga teacher in Bergedorf a suburb of Hamburg. Frederick knew the animosity the locals had against British civilians and sailors often leading to verbal duels. A lot was no doubt based on the defeat of the Nazi regime and the suffering of those that survived. There was remarkable growth and the manufacturing units were back in place after the devastation of the war. Frederick Stoldt went about his mission with great dedication.

He spent the whole day understanding the problems. Emma told him about the presence of some persons from a Russian agency that wielded great power with the police and the establishment. He was keen to unravel the Russian angle if any in the attacks against the members of Kosmica. He spent three days during which he was able to obtain the information that the Soviet secret agency was present in most cities in West Germany and wielded sufficient clout to get things done their way. He luckily met a German girl who was friendly with a Russian official that was from the secret agency. She understood his need for information inputs regarding the attitude of the Russian agency towards spiritualists. She was herself a researcher in ancient history of religions and was aware of the spiritual aspect. He returned to London and reported his findings to Bainbridge who was impressed with Stoldt's work. The other members of the team completed their individual assignments and impressed Bainbridge with their efficiency and acumen.

CHAPTER 27

Istanbul

Carlos guided by the Arrow now saw the unlikely scene of two persons of different religious backgrounds united by the fine thread of spiritualism.

"There are misguided humans today that wish to kill all those practicing spiritualism irrespective of their religious backgrounds. The teacher has already said we must came together and share our unique powers to defeat this menace by peaceful methods, not ruling out other means if unavoidable."

Thus spoke the Indian master of the Rishi tradition to his friend a master from Spain of the Assisi tradition in Istanbul in Turkey where a ghastly act of violence had taken the lives of a number of Dervishes.

They had both traveled to Istanbul through the astral path.

"Let's get started with Daniel's plan. We need to contact all grand masters and senior masters of all religious traditions and schools without exception from Buddhism, Judaism, Hinduism, Christianity, Islam, Taoism, Shintoism, Zoroastrianism as well as the Shomyo chanters of Japan, Shamans, Mantra chanters and many others oriented to realize the supra-physical potential of the human body and the human mind"

"Daniel wants us to achieve this without any loss of time?"

"We reach each of the selected ones telepathically and use astral travel"

"Who indeed are the selected ones and what made you select them?"

"I have selected them by using supra-visualization"

"Fine, let me then get to mentally transferring their identity from your mind bank to mine right this minute and proceed to advise them of your plan."

"How?"

"By mind mail. I will also organize our messengers some of whom will use telepathy and some will actually pursue astral travel for contacting the chosen ones."

A list of a total of one hundred seventy masters, grandmasters and others were contacted out of which at least a hundred forty to hundred fifty could finally make it. A core group of senior masters were identified and given the assignment of organizing this conclave once the location was determined by the teacher.

CHAPTER 28

London

Carlos viewed the night activity of a hireling of the cleanser organization thanks to the help of the Arrow.

The time was past eleven at night. Signs of intoxication were showing up on some of the pub crawlers while others were into serious binge drinking. The tight and randy were looking for night stands. Call girls were out on the streets busy luring tipsy males into splurging their lolly. Some chaps low on cash, were busy bargaining for price cuts. A half drunken man exclaimed to no one in particular

"Blimey I'd rather go home than bed these wretched bitches"

"Better you run off home and take your damned dick with you, you scum bag" came the reply.

Tom Bernard a small time crook and sharp shooter specializing in contract jobs for killing or maiming of targeted men or women was nervous. He was given the time of midnight to meet the client at a London pub. He did not know the client. He was to go, identify and meet the client who would be wearing a beret and sitting at a table close to the main bar. A further sign was to be a typical Scottish muffler in red color with checks wrapped round his neck. Tom reached the pub a bit before midnight sat on a barstool and called for a lime and lager his favorite liquid refreshment. After sipping his beer for a few minutes he walked slowly across to the gents' loo while taking a good look at the rest of the crowd in the pub to see if he could spot his man. There were two of them with Scottish mufflers but only one sported a beret. He kept going to avoid any suspicion. Emerging from the washroom he made a beeline to the man with the beret.

"Wonder if I could join you with my drink" he said to the man bowing slightly.

"Where is it?" asked the man.

"You mean the drink. It's right there. I'll join you in a minute" Tom fetched his beer and sat down at the man's table. He was pretty glad he spotted the man without much ado. The man turned out to be an aristocratic guy in his early fifties drinking expensive scotch on the rocks.

"Are you the one sent by Preserve Corporation?"

"Yes. Aren't you Mr. Wilson?"

"That's right."

"What's the job sir?"

"Elimination. The person is a Mr. Bainbridge. The details and the photo are in this envelop"

"Thanks. I'll do the needful"

"I've paid for two operatives plus the contract price"

"I'm only to get the info. The office guys do the planning and the quote"

"Fine. I'd have to leave" said the man with the beret getting up.

"It's O.K. with me. I'd have to get back home too"

Tom waited till the man left.

Tom was glad the meeting was productive. He quickly gulped his beer and left the pub.

CHAPTER 29

London

Carlos guided by the Arrow now gets to observe the covert preparations of the cleanser henchmen.

The 9.15 local from Heathrow stopped at Russell Square station where George Black alighted to meet his mentor Tom Bernard who was already there waiting. They took the escalator exiting at the south corner and went across to 'The Horizon' a not so expensive' hotel at the end of the street before Holborn station. They had not exchanged a word. Tom went to the counter and obtained the key to room 216 on the second floor which they quietly entered closing the door. "Have you got your gun?"

"Yes and also the curved kukri"

"Good, I have my weapons with me. Our action starts tomorrow. The target is at Princess Road. We are to reach there by train separately at around12.30 and go across to the offices of Ray, Boyd & Chester and take out a guy called Bainbridge whose photograph is with me. Take a look." Tom showed the photo.

"I know him. I saw him at Wesley hall along with many others that came to hear someone called John Sherman. This man accompanied Sherman"

"Why were you there?"

"I was on assignment to photograph as many participants as I could and get their names and other details."

"Good. That makes it easier. He has a meeting with a dame called Margie Boyd the managing partner of the law firm at one p.m. tomorrow. Our instructions are clear. We wait for Bainbridge and get him either

113

before or after his meeting with her. I go upstairs to do the job. You are to stay down. Should I miss out for any reason, you are to get him before he gets into his car.

"I know. We communicate by phone and keep our escape routes open."

"A car will be waiting at Kilburn Park station for me and another one for you at Queens Park."

"We take our independent approaches and get our cars ready and waiting at locations we choose and we get away immediately."

"We do not talk to each other except by phone ignoring to look at or recognize one another."

"We are not to wear bright colors" Perfect. Let's proceed and prepare for it." I think we better have a drink or something and stay here for a little while to avoid suspicion." "We do not use room service. We stay here for some time and each of us leaves separately. You leave first." "Done" Bainbridge sat in meditation. He started with ritual breathing and chanting of a favorite mantra from the book of sacred chants. He passed into a state of intense awareness and visualization. He saw two persons getting off the yellow line tube of the London underground rail network. They were both young, English and armed. Bainbridge increased his level of concentration and was able to foresee the intended activity of the duo. He continued with his meditation for a time and relaxed back to his normal activity. He spoke to Margie on the phone." This is Brian here. I have a request. Shall we have a meeting today somewhere away from your office to discuss a new project I have?""Certainly, tell me where and I'll be there. By the way, what happens to our meeting at my office tomorrow fixed for one p.m.?""That will stand. I'm starting here in ten minutes and will call you. I do not intend to take more than a half hour for the meeting and it will be some place near your office. "Alright, I await your call" Margie Boyd finished up with the brief she was dictating which Joyce her secretary would later unravel from the Dictaphone and neatly type out and place on her desk by the afternoon the same day. As she was putting on her coat, the call from Brian came and she went out to get her car, parked in the special parking lot reserved for partners of the firm. Bainbridge met her at Mabel's Bistro on Cambridge Street, a comfortable restaurant where people could talk with their privacy assured. "I have vital information that two hit men will attempt an attack on me tomorrow at your office when I come there for that pre-arranged meeting with you around one p.m. First you have to discretely find out how this meeting detail could have leaked out. Secondly I want a counter plan to be put in place to nab them, interrogate and obtain information about the people involved in the plot.""I'm with you. I'm afraid Joyce keeps my appointments diary in the Partners' common room which can be accessed quite easily by anyone who wants to check. I'll henceforth try to ensure that the meetings diary is kept inaccessible to others. Please go ahead and device a plan to nab these criminals and I'll assist in all possible ways.""I have a simple plan and it is this" Bainbridge explained the plan in detail to Mrs. Boyd who listened with utmost attention. It was agreed that they would keep things under wraps and put the plan into action for the likely events of the next day.

CHAPTER 30

London

Carlos through the Arrow observes the assassination attempt of the cleansers hired killers.

"I'm in position and watching the entrance"
"I'm inside the building'
"Should I call you on sighting the target?"
"No need. Be prepared in case I miss the target"
"Roger. Over and out for now."
Operation 'Elimination' was on.

They were at work at Princess Street. They had left their cars with instructions to the respective drivers to keep the engines running for a quick getaway

Bainbridge had his master plan all worked out. Stoldt and Graham had been briefed and detailed to cover the building dressed in somewhat disheveled clothes. While Graham stayed down, Stoldt went up to the law office and sat down purportedly waiting for Richard Chester. Richard Chester was taken into confidence about the murder plot and was asked to stay out of the office after informing Joyce the receptionist of his intention to be out for a while and that a certain gentleman wearing crumpled clothes would come for him who should be told to wait along with any other new clients that may come for him.

Tom with his gun well hidden entered the office of Ray, Boyd & Chester, the law firm. Gaining entrance to the reception area was pretty easy. There were other clients already waiting. He smiled at a person who looked somewhat disheveled and eased himself into the sofa next to him.

"Excuse me are you waiting to see Mrs. Boyd?"

"It's Mr. Chester I'm waiting to see"

"Is he out?"

"Indeed. He's expected soon"

Tom was relieved. The man never asked him about why he was there.

The receptionist was an attractive lady in her late forties and was immersed in her work which suited Tom. He had no way of knowing that the lady had prior instructions to discretely phone Mrs. Boyd if someone who was not a regular client came into the office.

Tom walked up to the lady saying "Good day Madam"

"Good day Sir. Did you want to see Mrs. Boyd?"

"No. I came for Mr. Chester"

"O.K, you'll have to wait a bit. He's expected to come at any moment. There's someone already waiting. Please be seated."

"Thanks" Tom was relieved.

He knew Mrs. Boyd was waiting to meet Bainbridge. He was prepared to shoot Bainbridge dead immediately as he entered the reception and quickly escape back to the waiting getaway car of his.

The receptionist never bothered to phone Mrs. Boyd about the visitor since he hadn't come for Mrs. Boyd.

Bainbridge in disguise was already in the office having entered through the staircase at the rear and sat in Chester's chamber without even the receptionist know it.

He asked Margaret "has any one come for you yet?"

"Apparently no, I've instructed Joyce to discretely phone me if anyone other than a regular client came to see me." She said

"That doesn't include those who may come to visit your partners. Does it?"

"I'm afraid not. I didn't think of it."

"Why don't you do it now?"

"O.K, Let me try."

Margaret rang Joyce. "Is any new client waiting for Richard?"

"Yes there's a new client come to see Mr. Chester"

"Describe him."

Joyce did as best as she could. Margaret conveyed it to Bainbridge.

"Ask Joyce to go to the new client and anyone else waiting for Mr. Chester and lead them to the briefing room and seat them there.

Let Leslie Serve them tea or coffee. He will know what to do" said Bainbridge.

The advice was conveyed to Joyce and as a result the new client and the other person, who was wearing a somewhat crumpled jacket, were shown into the Briefing room.

"Would you gentlemen have some tea or would you prefer coffee?"

Both opted for coffee with cream and were promptly served by Leslie the office assistant one cup at a time. Bainbridge was able to drug the coffee that went to Tom Bernard. Tom was nonplussed and did not want to sit in the room and miss out on getting a shot at Bainbridge. He got up and wanted to go back to the reception area after drinking his coffee but felt muddled and had to fall back in the sofa. The other person who actually was Stoldt in disguise promptly took him into custody and took away the gun that Tom had in a holster under the armpit.

Tim Graham and Sui Wu were trying to fulfill their assigned task of apprehending one of the assassins. They knew that two men were involved in the operation and both would have arranged getaway cars with their engines running. Since the main assassin was trying to kill the target in the law office, he would naturally have the getaway vehicle nearest to the entrance area of the building. Graham thinking logically was inclined to search for such a vehicle which invariably had to be a car with a driver sitting in it with his hand on the steering wheel, ready to take off when the right person entered it. He spotted it. The next thing was to spot the second vehicle. He and Sue went about it systematically doing a reconnaissance exercise. They were successful. The suspect car was parked about a hundred yards away in front of a Deli joint with its engine running, a burly man sitting at the wheel. Tim put into effect his 'side entrance technique' and stormed into the car poking his gun at the driver's back.

"Don't try any stunts. I will shoot to kill."

Sue entered from the front coming next to the driver. She went about immobilizing the driver with deft moves sealing his mouth with tape and tying up his hands and feet. Tim got the driver to sit on the floor while Sue eased herself into the driver's seat. Tim sitting at the rear was ready with the gun and was prepared to tackle the assassin as and when he showed up.

George Black was jittery. There was no sign of the target and no communication from Bernard and it was past the scheduled meeting time. He sensed that something was amiss. He quickly walked back to the getaway car from the elevator bay in the lobby of the building where he was keeping watch. He opened the car door only to be roughly pulled in.

Tim pointed his gun at the man and Sue did the rest. She took away the assassin's gun and repeated the operation of sealing his mouth and tying him up securely.

The two assassins were interrogated by Bainbridge and it turned out that they had been hired by a front organization of the underworld called 'Investigators & Security suppliers plc' with an address in central London. The agency had assigned them to interact with a client who would instruct them. The client had already paid a huge sum for the services including elimination of a Londoner. They had no idea as to who commissioned them to murder Bainbridge except for their handler client who never appeared to them face to face but only passed on instructions by phone.

Bainbridge decided to tackle the underworld agency later but meanwhile had the police take charge of the two operators. Meanwhile efforts were to be started to identify the Cleanser network.

Various teams of protectors were going through similar exercises in various parts of the world. The targeted spiritualists were being saved by the protector teams. Yet it was not enough, it seemed.

CHAPTER 31

Cairo

Carlos guided by the Arrow observes the description of how a get together of the spiritual masters was being planned.

"It is a unique and a highly guarded secret meeting of eminent mystics of the world now set to happen at a top secret location" said the Sufi master.

"What about their background? Will the spiritual masters and grandmasters forget their strong sectarian hang ups? Maybe you could please educate me on the whole thing" said the disciple.

"The main and only goal of this get together is to evolve a common approach to the danger of obliteration by the evil brigade known as 'Cleansers International' that had suddenly become a menace to all those that are into spiritual practices of varied intensities and effects. The cleansers are propagating the idea that the spiritualists were anti god and anti religion and that they opposed the word of God revealed directly and through the archangels and through avatars of the supreme. By misleading the masses the cleansers are hopeful of alienating them from the influence of these spiritual masters. The mystics as you know were time and time again deemed by some religious fundamentalists as blasphemers deserving to be put to death on sight. The cleansers are trying to cash in on this sentiment"

"Please tell me about how the masses see the different sects and your own view of them"

"The mainly Jewish Kabbalah came into its own when the king of Spain had banished its members. Strangely the Sultan of Turkey had given them shelter. The Yogis and Mahatmas of India, the Ahl-al-Haqiqah saints of Sufi Islam, the ascended masters of the Kabbalah, the Medicis and mystics of Christianity, the Bodhisattvas of Buddhist lore and many others like the Munis of Jainism were all rebels that were shunned by the priests and scholars. They established the fact that erudition and intellectual brilliance do not always lead to divine experience or vision of the kingdom of god within oneself."

"How do you say that"

"Great prophets and messiahs had all gathered simple folk such as fishermen, shepherds or farmers as disciples and gave them power and made those great. Whom did Jesus choose into his inner circle? Not the intellectuals or nobles or priests. It was the same with Buddha who had Upali, a barber leading the Sangha. Mahavira and Nanak had done likewise."

"Tell me. Are you excited to be in the conclave of these grand masters and masters?"

"I cannot even convey a hundredth of what I feel. It is exhilarating to see the manner in which the masters are keen to set about the task. Instant and effective empowerment is sought to be implemented without considering the tradition the masters evolved themselves from. Hinduism Islam Christianity Buddhism Jainism and all other backgrounds will hold no importance. A Sufi saint would gladly empower a Christian cabala adherent to levitate or vice versa. A Hindu Mahan would gladly empower a Zoroastrian Master to dematerialize and rematerialize to facilitate instant change of location. For perhaps the first time since humans came into existence there is this phenomenal bonding of all spiritual masters for a common purpose of ensuring the well being of humanity and the world. A team of four super masters under the guidance of Daniel will head the entire campaign and device the methods and the action needed to transform the cleansers into normal humans.

It has been agreed that there is to be no argument between the spiritualists among themselves about the way the universe operates. That is a strict rule never to be broken. Once the conclave of grandmasters takes its decisions on all issues, many young men and women will receive special training and empowerment in various centers across the world.

At the end of the day the most important aspect of the bonding will be the creation of a super league of young intelligent men and women drawn from different backgrounds for countering the cleansers. The league will have definite goals and the emphasis is to be on utilizing the right means with no trace of hatred except the highest degree of commitment to restore spiritual ideals and values back into the society. To this end several contingents of young men and women members of the league that are already advanced in their practices attaining considerable energy quotient are to receive training. They will be initiated by the grand masters into attaining supra—human capabilities".

"Such as for example"

"Such as the power to disappear and remain invisible, the power to fly, the power to immobilize a body or object from a distance, the power to visualize a situation and read the minds of others at will and the power to create means instantly to be used against a person or an object. The empowerment is to be so initiated as to have a 'one member one power' norm. Thus the league of young men and women who would be specially trained by the grandmasters will collectively have powers to deal with any situation. These contingents are to be authorized to lock horns with those evil cleansers that are out to destroy the spiritualists."

"What happens next?"

"I would say a lot is going to happen and the empowered men and women are set to transform the so called cleansers by their superior strategy of confronting and proving a few things."

"Such as"

"The utter uselessness of the cleansers' temporal powers namely the power of money, weapons or networking."

"What will be the result?"

"Complete transformation of those who at this point in time oppose spirituality into convinced supporters of all that is spiritual"

"Within what time frame would you say?"

"I would say less than three years for us in the western hemisphere"

"Fair enough let's hope so"

"However there is something sinister that the cleansers are trying to do to discredit the spiritual masters"

"Such as what for instance?"

"Propagating stories of Sexual misbehavior on trumped up charges or of corruption, both very potent instruments to discredit the masters and grand masters and others. Men and women are being recruited as mercenaries on a grand scale for use as decoys and false accusers for this sinister purpose"

"God save them. Human history is full of betrayers and traitors."

"One more thing"

"What?"

"The cleansers are zeroing in on to the forbidden zone. They have identified the person that has the power to enter a higher dimension. They are trying to kill him or perhaps may have already killed him."

"Who is the person?"

"An Indian businessman called Hazrara"

"The grandmasters, will they not take care of the situation?"

"I'm afraid it isn't that easy"

"Why?"

"The cleansers it appears have roped in a spiritual grand master of great power to help them"

"Who is he?"

"No one is prepared to reveal. It is their top secret"

"It is so unfortunate. History tells us of many such spiritual grand masters. They fall prey to jealousy and egoism despite their exalted stature. Even the great Buddha had to contend with his own jealous cousin Deavadatta that tried to get him killed."

"Let's hope we will be able to get over the hassle"

CHAPTER 32

London

*Carlos guided by the Arrow gets to see the strange confrontation
of the empowered ones with the cleansers in London.*

The grand master Parama gave Bainbridge the freedom to pick his
team for direct action apart from the international back up available from
groups associated with the great master's work of ensuring world harmony
and peace. Bainbridge along with Bose and Mason put the combined

B-7 team into several intensive training sessions for three weeks and
found them excellent in the required skills of alacrity, grasping power,
quick—response capability and unflinching dedication to the job at hand.

Meanwhile at the instance of his leader Dimitriev, Malankayev
arrived in London with his gang of killer thugs. An 'action plan session'
was held at an exclusive hotel cum safe house in the regent street area
where a team of twelve men sat down to discuss and formulate the
logistics of carrying out violent and deadly operations.

"Our latest information indicates that the big man is scheduled to
lecture on his pet subject this Monday week at a venue that is well known
to us"

"You mean Parama is to lecture on the subject of his spiritual
humbug"

"I think it's best to avoid names and subjects in our business. All of
us are aware of what I'm talking about. I suggest we form ourselves into
groups and strike simultaneously at this venue plus three other places to
achieve a sensational serial massacre that'll create shock ripples across the
world"

"Let's do it perfectly this time" said the gang in one voice.

"The best way is to first target the congregation and then move on to the celebrities sitting on the podium."

"I couldn't agree with you more" said Malankayev. He formed four teams of three persons each.

Discussions and consultations followed for two days after which plans were finalized and tasks allotted and arrangements made for the distribution of weapons and ammunition. The logistics of travel to designated places were also put in place.

Bainbridge had specific insights of the sinister plans of the cleanser gang. He had Mason set up a secret get together of the B-7 team. It took place in the Bishops gate area in a safe apartment in London's Grace Church Street.

Along with Mason, the B-7 team headed by Bose was informed by Bainbridge of the impending danger of attack by the Cleansers. "They are out to create a panic situation by carrying out attacks at three or more places. They would target the congregations to kill the maximum number of people" said Bainbridge and added "We are meeting our grandmaster Parama right here in this house for a session of empowerment. Each of you will receive certain spiritual powers for use to effectively counter the actions of the attackers. There will be no need for you to kill or maim the attackers. This is in accordance with our sacred creed of not taking human life at anytime despite facing the worst provocation".

"May we if necessary use our martial-arts skills to contain them?" asked Bose.

"Yes of course without doubt" assured Bainbridge.

"Now I would like to leave you here tonight to get some sleep and to mentally prepare yourselves for the initiation."

The Initiation by Parama happened the next morning. Parama looked at each one of them affectionately at first and spoke with firmness and clarity. "As Bainbridge may have told you, we are passing through strange and dangerous times. There is need for each of you to understand that physical strength alone may not suffice to counter these well trained and armed killers or assassins who are at this very moment perhaps roaming around in London like their associates are doing in other cities across Britain and Europe. They are looking for persons who according to them are spiritually oriented meaning those practicing yoga, meditation, chanting and so on. I now wish to give each one of you certain powers to last for a temporary period till the cleanser menace is over and done with. After that you will have to evolve spiritually to be able to retain the powers that you are now receiving"

Parama temporarily empowered the B-7 members after a special process of intensive mind-intellect-indoctrination with certain new memory inputs unrelated to their own thought processes and normal memory skills. The empowerment gave powers such as disappearance at will, using counter pressure against the opponent's attacking weapons and the ability to dominate the opponent's thought patterns causing mental derangement and confusion.

"Interesting results are bound to come when the opposition is confronted" Parama said.

The confrontation happened pretty soon thereafter.

The first team of the cleansers targeted the venue of Parama's lecture at the main hall of the International conference centre close to Westminster abbey.

Bainbridge now assigned the task of defense plus counter-action to Bose, Stoldt and Shalini. They positioned themselves at strategic locations at the conference venue.

Malankayev had decided to lead the attack along with three other of his henchmen at this venue while his other teams proceeded to three other locations in London, the first and second close to the railroad stations of Charing Cross and the Queen's and the third at the Strand.

Bose opted to be close to Parama while Stoldt and Shalini were at the entrance of the main hall with some distance between them. The others in the B-7 placed themselves at the three other places of impending cleanser attack.

Before the start of the function Parama was introduced to the large audience by the secretary of the sponsors namely the 'Civil Society for Advancement'.

'Dear friends it is a great moment for us today. The great man, I'm sure you know who I'm referring to, has agreed to address us. He makes it appear as though he is as ordinary as any one of the millions of people that inhabit our planet. It is his modesty and his spiritual level and his divinity that sets him apart. Almost everyone here I'm sure will agree with me and fully appreciate his uniqueness. Without wasting anymore time, I feel highly honored and have the greatest of pleasure in presenting him to you. I now most humbly request our Mr. Parama to address us.

Parama got up and started his address.

"Dear friends and fellow spiritualists I extend my warm greetings and good wishes to each one of you. I normally stay away from conferences and gatherings since I always feel that I'm not qualified nor have I any special knowledge to give advice or have important insights to share with others whom I consider to be fellow travelers in this journey of life. By believing in the benefits of spiritualism of thought and action, I feel we perhaps end up enjoying our journey a little more than those who do not care to so believe. However I am here speaking to you today to convey the message of how important it is for all of us to stand firm and united against the persecution with its violent sword of hatred that has recently been let loose. These brothers intend to eliminate all of us spiritualists around the world. It is a matter of irony that we who passionately desire peace, harmony and happiness for all humanity have been targeted in this cruel manner."

"Why do you think they are doing this?" asked a delegate.

"I'm not sure. All I can say is that we have to patiently and with love try and correct these brothers of ours"

Parama went on to explain the concepts of spiritual practitioners who consider all actions equally important in human lives there being nothing which is considered big or small per se.

Parama spoke for an hour. Thankfully there was no disturbance or violence at this venue.

The reason was simple and interesting. Malankayev was in camouflage dressed as a regular bobby from the London police. Bainbridge who had confronted Malankayev earlier was alert and ready. He became invisible and dealt most suitably with Malankayev. He first grabbed and pulled out the two pistols that Malankayev carried in holsters attached to his belts worn around the waist and across the shoulder resulting in utter awe and shock for him. Bainbridge later had the police commissioner expose Malankayev as a fake officer of the London police. Malankayev's associates meanwhile were countered by Bose and his team even before they reached their vintage points by a series of swift kungfu maneuvers coupled with body punches that incapacitated them temporarily. Further drama was added by confusing their thought process resulting in their roaming around outside the main hall as though utterly lost and disoriented all of which saved the day. Malankayev was let off by the police after a warning since he used no weapons and had stated that it was all a prank for which he was sorry.

Malankayev's other teams had similar experiences with the B-7 members dealing with them. However the massacre of spiritualists in Liverpool and Manchester at around the same time accounting for the death of fifteen persons and injuries to many more, as quoted in the newspapers, distressed Parama, Bainbridge and others beyond measure. They realized that Kosmica did not have enough people to cover all places in all towns in all countries.

CHAPTER 33

Helsinki/ Helsingfors, Finland

Carlos with the Arrow's guidance and commentary goes back in time to observe the childhood and the subsequent role of a beautiful Indian girl called Veena working for Kosmika.

The place was a small town in South India. A British gentleman was walking along a dirt road. The year was 1940.

A pleasant smile of anticipation spread over his face when he thought of her. He was going to see her today. He started walking briskly on the crude country road red with mud. The rain had stopped. Wasn't much of a rain though? All the same it did help to ease the sweltering heat a wee bit and thus was welcome. The road criss-crossed for the most part amidst little puddles of muddy water where an occasional buffalo would stretch its neck and drink. More water in the paddy fields, not as mucky really, having stood for some time clearing itself in the bargain. Little huts of bamboo with palm-leaf roofs stood in disarranged rows with ample open space between them on all sides. Dotted occasionally here and there were comfortable bungalows made of brick and stone. The bungalows usually had a front garden with lawns on either side of an impressive drive way. The gardens in turn were usually well tended with neat orderly rows of marigolds, roses and other flower plants and shrubs. The crowded market place or bazaar and the thickly populated residential quarters of the hoi polloi and the small huts for the outcastes were spread out elsewhere in this small town. He was used to all this, the coexistence of opulence and downright squalor. It wasn't easy at first. But it was rather surprising how years of intimacy with the surroundings robbed one of wonder or shock. All the same he liked this country now with all its contradictions. Sentimental? Well what the heck, why not, he thought.

James Christopher Jones or "Jones Dora" as people called him here in these parts, had reasons to be happy and joyful. It was surprising how apart from their own native bosses the locals called the Whiteman a 'Dora' which in the local lingo actually meant 'Lord' or 'Ruler'. Somehow thanks to the machinations of a colonial regime, any individual of European origin if male was deemed to represent a ruling class person just as any member of the local caste 'Velama Dora'. Just fancy that. "Me a Lord, for Christ's sake, never, not on your life, I Just wouldn't have it' thought Jones. His father was a farmer and a proud one at that. 'Lord' indeed he said to himself "Phew, striped trousers, frock coat, top hat and a carnation in the button—hole with lots and lots of ballyhoo and Ho Ha. Some of them, very few indeed perhaps real dunderheads. Well let them enjoy. What does it matter as long as things kept glowing back home" said Jones sotto voce.

Jones kept walking. He liked it better than traveling by his car driven by the prim and properly dressed official chauffer.

What might Veena be doing? Hope she is at home though. Her long coal black hair and those large innocent impish eyes and the upturned nose. Coming to think of it, an upturned nose wasn't all that common here in this part of the world. England? Well yes but not out here. Then again India surely was a country of surprises. Color as understood back home didn't seem to work here at any rate. Some were as fair and light skinned as white men and women and some as dark as Africans sometimes in the same family with a variety of intermediate shades. Mildred bless her was so very understanding. Always cheerful she never once wanted to go back home. Well there's no denying it. One did long for one's own surroundings as Shakespeare said somewhere "This heaven on earth this England". England, a beautiful place really; ought to be reading Shakespeare more. Twenty-five years now. A long time by any standard, but no regrets no regrets at all. Strange how his wife Mildred was excited and thrilled as a young bride at the prospect of coming all the way to India, the jewel in the monarch's crown. Mildred and he, they loved each other. No doubt about that. That spark was still there. Thank heavens it'll always be there. He had been plain lucky. That's all. She hated parties as much as he did. The parties where inevitably all those old songs were sung in rooms with false fire places with no fires burning, Lime and lager, gin and tonic or scotch and soda with lots of ice or on the rocks, drinks that weren't too wholesome and those wines with exotic names bottled in France, roast beef and Yorkshire pudding among other things on the table. Well that was an effort to create an ambience of 'home'. Perhaps for a moment all the colonial gents and ladies instantly got transported to their places in Britain that great country, the Island Nation that ruled the world together with Germany, France, Portugal and Holland, colonizing at will. Then there were those flirtations to overcome the boredom. Mildred dear girl never looked at another man ever. What a relief. 'I was equally faithful 'never had eyes for any other', yes, he cared only for her.

The sun was going down and such beautiful crimson splashing around, red road, red sky and all a glorious red! Twenty-five years of sunshine could be a bit much and too damn hot in summer and it was summer most of the time in the south here wasn't it? One could always escape to some hill station or to places like Darjeeling or Shimla or Shrinagar in the north where there was snow fall in winter, thought he.

Jones progressed at a much slower pace now. He stopped at a big bungalow painted chalk white. Just imagine someone painting the house chalk white in England. His eyes fell on the gardener or 'Mali' as he was called here. The Mali with his face like a mask wished him respectfully although surprised that he came walking and not in his car. He held the gate open. Jones entered the house past the wooden gate and involuntarily looked up and there was Veena, little Veena staring wondrously from behind the huge window through the iron bars across it. These windows with iron bars ever so grim making it seem more like a Calaboose.

Veena caught sight of Jones and her face was pure joy. She turned and ran down the stairs jumping and skipping shouting at the top of her voice "Tella Mamayya" "Tella Mamayya" and the next minute she had caught hold of his hand and was pulling him into the house. For a four year old, the world with all its mystery and wonderment just lurking around the corner must still seem pretty simple. She called Jones 'Tella mamayya' white-uncle as he was much whiter than daddy and all the other uncles and certainly much more likeable than all her other uncles. Well as a matter of fact she liked him as well as she liked Daddy and Tella Mamayya was nearly as tall as daddy. Oh! Daddy was so awfully tall and to have to look all that high to see whether he was angry or kind.

Jones remembered how Veena as a tiny one year old had cried when he tried to kiss her the first time. Well you couldn't blame her, could you? Big blinking moustaches and a beet root face, must have terrified her surely. After a couple of times the ice was broken and familiarity grew. It was rather difficult to fathom how it all really happened. Jones as a rule wasn't too fond of children. Well, he didn't detest the little brats but again wasn't fond of them either. It never did really seem to matter not having children of his own. Mildred may have wanted them at first but their love for each other had never suffered because of lack of them. Somehow Veena was different. She touched the innermost depths of those hidden layers of tenderness and there sprang forth a flood of affection. Quite inexplicable it was.

Veena's father Raghav was an unusually tall and dignified man in his late thirties, spoke excellent English, looked one straight in the eye and got on splendidly with others especially with white Europeans. He was pleasant to look at and had natural charm that man, his English diction as good as any of the Oxford boys; Sincere and capable too, worked his way right up to the top, yes sir to the very top. Yet Jones was still the numero uno in the outfit. Well it was the policy laid down for all departments of administration in keeping strictly with the British colonial dictum 'thus far and no further' for the natives that were to adorn at most the second rung in the hierarchy. This was the rule in the provinces in India called presidencies pre-fixed by the name of the principal city of the region such as Madras or Bombay which were under the direct administration of the British colonial power. Jones was not in agreement with this patent discrimination but was shrewd enough to realize that governance of a huge country like India wasn't easy for a tiny nation like Britain of the Ingles, Scots, the Welsh and perhaps the Irish among others who nursed grudges against one another at home. The only way was to follow the dictum of those who knew what they were doing, meaning the true 'Empire builders.' India indeed was a strange country with its people having no common rallying point. It had divisions galore by way of language, religion and many other things. The Hindu religion had its own extra dimensions of caste, social status and race. The powerful ruling elite of the Muslims that was dominant in the north and the center was not so now. The Sikhs and the Marathas were claiming total control in parts of the country when the British entered India which then was a vast conglomerate of independent kingdoms. The British 'shop-keepers' however had matured into political masters and colonists and many years had to pass and many disparate Indian groups like the Sikhs and the Gorkhas had to expend enormous muscle power working as soldiers in the British Indian Army to help consolidate British rule over most of

India while the Maharajas and Nawabs continued to rule their various kingdoms with British regents in place.

The British certainly had anxious moments, what with those freedom movements and jail-going by all and sundry. Yet one had to be fair. They did encourage and give posts of authority to the natives. The British had given the Indians a fool proof civil-service and a judiciary which certainly was a help. Well may be Britain did milk something out of India and what do you expect? Come all the way for tweedle—dum. Have a heart. Well the least said about it the better. What after all is a couple of hundred years in the history of mankind? Look at America. Look at it. One has to learn to live and let live. It won't do getting worked up and punching people in the face. Come to think of it, the British in Asian colonies must say are different from the folks back home. None of that open hearted simplicity and the grin over a 'pint of draught' or 'lime and lager' in the 'Pig and Whistle' back home. One couldn't control a colony that way could he? A bit bigoted may be like the Klu Klux Klan boys. No wonder the natives make faces, Jones said sotto voce.

For Jones today his immediate concern was his impending departure from this strange, colorful and glorious country. Normally after retirement the District Collectors, magistrates and other white men in superior positions inevitably left India to go back home to England or Wales or Scotland or the Isle of Wight or wherever. For some unknown reason Mildred and Jones decided on going back to the Isle of Wight years before Jones was to retire. The British administration had promised to accommodate Jones at an appropriate level in its civil service network back home to give him time to settle down thus relieving him of any worry. The Isle of Wight looked as promising as any other to Jones since he had an old relative living there, his own parents having passed away while he was serving the 'British Raj' in India.

Today Jones thought he would have some enjoyable time with Veena and her family and would invite them over to his own bungalow for the big party on Saturday after which he and Mildred were scheduled to leave for England. They would first get to Bombay by train and board the 'Empress Victoria' a passenger ship of the British India Steam Navigation Company that would sail to England.

Before finally leaving India with Mildred, Jones felt he had to extract a promise from Raghav that he would keep in regular touch and to ensure that Veena visited them in the Isle of Wight at least once before she was married off to a suitable boy as was customary in this part of the world where marriages were meticulously arranged after checking out the horoscopes of the girl and the boy once their social status and caste were reconciled.

Veena led Jones in and he thoroughly enjoyed himself in the company of Raghav's household and left them after extending an invitation for them to come over to his bungalow on Saturday for the big party.

Mildred and James Christopher Jones left for Bombay two days after the big party bidding farewell to all their friends to finally board the ship for their journey homewards from Bombay. Jones and Mildred had not foreseen that India after the end of the Second World-war and a longish period of political unrest and uncertainty would in 1947 attain her independence and that all British administrators would be forced to leave except those in the Imperial Bank and the armed forces who would have the option to stay on to work with their new Indian masters.

Veena's father Raghav kept his bond with the Joneses that left India to settle in the Isle of Wight. The Joneses James and Mildred had no children and considered Veena as their own and insisted that Veena study in England at the main University at East Cowes in the Isle of Wight with them acting as her responsible and happy guardians. Veena a brilliant student graduated in geophysics with distinction from a college in India and went across to the Isle of Wight and obtained her master's degree in the same subject. It was unbounded joy for Mildred and James as well as for Veena who experienced the love of foster parents that had taken her to heart. Her smallest wish was an inviolable order for the Joneses. The two years of Veena's study at Queens University passed off like a sweet dream for the trio.

Raghav wanted Veena to get her doctoral degree but she wasn't too keen. She wanted work experience before attempting it. She took up a job with a company called 'Geo-consult' of London with offices worldwide. She was required to travel on company's work to various places in Europe

Veena, now a young maiden, exquisite in her beauty was standing in the Satamakatu area of Helsinki opposite a public phone booth waiting her turn to phone. She thought of the things that she went through in the past months.

The bilingual city of Helsinki also called Helsingfors would surprise anyone traveling through Finland on rail. For the most part of the rail journey one would see greenery and more greenery with a sprinkling of modest wooden houses at locations far removed from each other. When one finally gives up on finding anything close to a city with its bustle and hustle, there suddenly appears Helsinki the big city with all the trappings of a modern capital as a bit of a shock although a pleasant one nevertheless.

With picturesque beauty the streets crossing each other with sign boards splashing strange longish names, Helsinki made one feel amused and strangely calm. The Swedish Russian Finnish juxtaposition of street names based on Finland's history sometimes seemed confusing. The pace of life easygoing and relaxed added to the serenity. The shadow of the Soviet Union next door did not seem to have affected these fun loving people. Finns are fond of their Sauna joints, rolling in the snow and bathing naked in ice cold waters in chilly weather. Those who visit for the first time are amazed at the friendliness they encounter at every step in Finland.

It was a strange reason indeed that brought her to Helsinki. One would have to go back a little in time to appreciate the reason.

Building on the spiritual experiences she had in India, Veena came under the influence of the local chapter of 'Kosmica' and attended the meetings and workshops organized by it in the Isle of Wight and elsewhere in the British Isles whenever she could.

Veena was immensely impressed with Kosmica after she found out more about its origin.

She went into the early history of Kosmica and came to know how

Kosmica started in the United States during the second world—war years. The United States had not initially fully involved itself in the Second World War till the Japanese destroyed their Pearl Harbor complex by a pre-emptive strike. The Japanese men and women had been isolated across North America as a precautionary measure and the U. S. had lent its full support to the Allied forces that ultimately defeated the Axis combine. It was around this time that a Swami of the World Spiritual order for cosmic harmony based in Canada started uniting all spiritually inclined persons to sincerely pray for peace. Informal meetings were regularly held to orient people towards spiritualism and non violence. The movement spread rapidly and many congregations across Canada and North America came into being. Spiritual masters with special powers and capabilities came to be associated with the movement. Apart from prayer and yoga, the masters taught meditation techniques and mind control methods and slowly a committed leadership emerged in the organization. Given the extraordinary talent for organization and rapid expansion of activity of the Canadians and the Americans the movement was canalized under the name of Kosmica with regular offices and meeting places across the Americas.

Later it grew around the world particularly all over Europe.

Veena was aware right from her teens that the human brain had four divisions and each had a specific area of application and purpose, the last quarter being for past life memory and intuition related activity. She knew that the great sages of ancient India had established several areas of learning and fruitful action through a' meditation plus intuition' oriented process. Apart from the four Vedas that contained sections of intuitive knowledge attributed to some of the sages, the 'Yoga Sutras' of Patanjali that dealt with the scope and purpose of yoga and the 'Shiva-sutras' of Panini that established the rules of syntax and grammar for the Sanskrit language were believed to be so evolved. Veena was keen on understanding the realms beyond normal human brain activity and wished to access them through meditation same as the yogis and Rishis of the past.

The Joneses were regular church goers quite content with living their lives guided by the simple sermons of the padres not bothering to delve any deeper into the so called mysteries of where one came from and where one goes when one dies and so on. Veena never tried to disturb their simple religious ways. Though a Hindu she always felt at home attending church functions with great enthusiasm. She felt the atmosphere of reverent silence quite strange yet soothing. She tried understanding the belief of the Catholic Church in transubstantiation of wine and bread into the blood and flesh of Christ to be consumed by the devout. She was sure there was some deeper meaning in the belief of the faithful that was perhaps evident to those who analyzed and studied the messiah's crucifixion and resurrection. She inwardly felt that all religious beliefs ultimately evolved into spiritual mysticism leading to higher levels of understanding and towards mastering the hidden energy sources and magical powers ever present in our physical universe.

Veena shifted to London where she was posted by her company Geo-Consult, temporarily staying at a hotel while looking out for suitable paying guest accommodation or' digs' as one called it similar to 'La pensione's of Europe.

While in London Veena suddenly found herself drawn into a close circle of spiritual people as if by accident. On a Sunday while sitting at Trafalgar square looking at the famous landmarks, a teen age girl came and sat next to her and said "You are in danger. Please come with me.'

Veena was more amused than shocked. She asked in a perfectly normal tone 'How do you know? And what is the danger may I ask?'

'You are a member of Kosmika aren't you? They are killing members like you mercilessly'

'Who are they?' Veena shot back while getting up and accompanying the girl. 'How do you know I am with Kosmika?' she asked.

'You must trust me. I know. This is not the time to argue' she literally pulled Veena into a small sedan that had its engine running with another young girl at the wheel. As the car started to speed away there was the sound of a gunshot that just missed the car.

'I'm Jessica Jackson and this is Linda Smith at the wheel. We know you are Veena Raghav from the East Cowes in the Isle of Wight.'

Veena kept silent.

'I know you are confused. You heard the gunshot. It was meant for you'

'Thanks for saving my life' Veena said. Jessica wasn't sure she meant it.

The car stopped at a hotel in Russell Street and the trio got down and led by Jessica went up to the fifth floor to a room and rang the bell. A young girl admitted them into the room.

"This is Christine and this is Veena" Jessica introduced them.

It was a sitting room of a suite that led into a dining space and thence into a bedroom with an attached bath and a separate dressing enclosure. It was quite spacious and empty except for a carpet and a few chairs arranged in a circle.

"Linda Meyer is coming over. She knows that you two would bring Veena here" said Christine addressing Jessica.

"Who is Linda Meyer?" asked Veena.

"Oh, I forgot. She is part of B-7 that protects the spirituals; I mean those pursuing the path of yoga, meditation and so on"

Sure enough Linda walked in with Bose in tow.

A tête-à-tête followed lasting for an hour. Veena was impressed with what Bose told her and believed him. She agreed to stay in the hotel with the girls.

Bose had earlier received instructions from Kosmika to guard Veena as she had a special empowerment that she was not aware of but somehow was known to the cleansers.

Veena stayed at the hotel and was asked to keep her room locked and not to venture out without proper escort.

The very next day Veena woke up hearing a soft sound and was surprised to find a strange person standing in front looking at her with kindness and affection. She did not understand how he came in. The main door to the suite was closed and her own room locked from inside.

"Do not be alarmed dear sister. As a member of Kosmika you are aware of the many strange powers that Yoga bestows on those who practice it with focused devotion and discipline. I am Daniel a name I was given at birth."

Veena felt at ease and rather pleased to be in the stranger's company.

'What do you want from me Sir?"

"I came to awaken you to your empowerment and to assign you a task"

"What empowerment?"

"You are to understand some unique facts that I intend to tell you before going into other issues. May I sit down to start explaining?"

"Sorry. I forgot. Please do sit down on this chair."

There followed a long narration by Daniel which came as a huge surprise to Veena, the story sounding strange and bizarre.

"You will now go to Helsinki and do me the favor of using your considerable skills in flooring the opposition as also uncovering the renegade Yoga Master."

"Why Helsinki may I ask?"

"Certainly. A huge Cleanser network is in operation with Helsinki as a base. The main operators slip in and out of Russia. You are to break into their organization and provide them information which I will pass on to you. You have also to meet up with persons mentioned in my dossier. You will have to slip in and out of Russia for this purpose. Let me give you the necessary equipment and information."

Daniel handed over a set of envelopes with a folder containing several papers, travelers' checks and so on and departed saying "Be careful and keep in touch. You will receive instruction to gain the required powers from the person whose details are in the dossier."

Veena had taken the assignment with great enthusiasm and applied for leave to her company. Her employers Geo Consult granted her leave of absence for two months.

Veena reached Helsinki. She stayed in a modest hostel for women in central Helsinki. She routinely mingled with the other residents in the hostel and was successful in getting to know a Swedish girl that had a boyfriend called Karl Schumann. Veena had a doubt whether this Karl Schumann was the same one indicated in the dossier Daniel gave her.

After a while she came back from her reverie to the present when her turn at the phone booth came and she spoke to Daniel.

"I'm into investigating all relevant aspects. Please check out a person called Karl Schumann. I met him through his Swedish girl friend staying in my hostel. I am going across to St. Petersburg tomorrow. I met up with the Kabbalah master and he was very helpful. He will teach and initiate me into 'mind-mail' activity. I can then communicate with you freely without fear.

The cleanser network was superbly organized in Finland and its neighboring countries. Many youth clubs were opened with facilities for partying. Young and influential men and women were invited and offered membership with just a token subscription. As members they were ensured of having a good time with a lot of bonhomie and élan. The core group which was highly paid ran these clubs. As a secret mission each club recruited suitable men and women to form a separate group and trained them systematically for months before assigning them their tasks of eliminating the spiritual practitioners and their followers in Russia, Finland, Norway, Sweden and Denmark. There were frequent exchanges of members from similar clubs between these countries. There was a close knit intelligence network operating to identify the spiritualists and their meeting places. The actual killing operation was under the overall command of the Russian contingent headed by Nikolai Dimitriev.

CHAPTER 34

St. Petersburg

Carlos continues to observe movements and actions of Veena as guided by the Arrow.

Veena traveled to St. Petersburg. She read the history of the city located in the Gulf of Finland in the Baltic Sea and of how it was set up by Peter the Russian Tsar in 1703 and managed to remain the capital of the Russian empire for over 150 years. Also that It was known as Petrograd and Leningrad.

It was necessary for her to be discreet and secretive lest her mission get jeopardized.

She wore dark glasses and altered the color of her hair. Veena went to the Indian Consular office in the Tsentralny area where most countries had their consulates. She met up with the Indian Consul—General Mr.Pradip Kanda.

"I got a message from our Moscow headquarters that you are working for Geo-Consult from London and that Mr. Shasihaas our first secretary from the embassy in Moscow has been asked to provide you with information and assistance. He is presently here in St. Petersburg. You may if you like interact with him right away."

Shasihaas a thirty—five year old Indian diplomat working in the Soviet Union for the past two years hailed from Kerala, a state in India that usually was home for nearly twenty percent of the men and women posted in Indian missions around the world by the Indian Foreign Service.

Apart from his academic brilliance, Shasihaas was a superb tactician and a well informed person with a charming personality. He was also into spiritual practices.

The first meeting between Veena and Shasihaas was in one of the sound proof conference rooms of the Consulate that was routinely debugged from time to time.

"Mentor Daniel sent me here."

"I know. He spoke with me. We both are to be part of the team chosen to unravel some of the mysteries."

"One of them is to identity the renegade Spiritual yogi"

"Yes. Are you familiar with visualization techniques?"

"Luckily yes."

"In my previous session I saw a face that seemed Asian rather than European"

"I suggest we do a session together and get some clarity"

"Indeed why not? Let us start."

Veena and Shasihaas focused their minds and started their session.

"There's heavy blockage disturbing our concentration."

"I too feel it"

"Perhaps the yogi has blocked access. We better stop lest he visualizes our purpose and also identifies us"

"Yes, it could be dangerous, I know."

"I'm sure he will not escape identification. However let's contact Daniel before proceeding further".

Shasihaas contacted Daniel.

"I'm glad you have identified the yogi's general area of origin. One has to study the lists of all the recognized spiritual masters of the various religious backgrounds based in Asia. I know it's difficult but can be done. Let me try to do it and get back. I would suggest that you draw a resemblance of the type of the face you saw in your visualization so that we may try and pin down the rogue grandmaster's ethnicity. By the way let Veena have a word with me" said Daniel to Shasihaas.

Veena contacted Daniel.

"Veena, listen carefully. I have checked out Karl Schumann. He is the one mentioned in the dossier. Do be very alert. You have to penetrate the group without giving any reason for them to suspect your identity. They should know that you are a spiritual practitioner. Before you take them on, you start with the Kabbalah master and become mind mail savvy as quickly as possible" Daniel told Veena.

There was a sense of bonhomie and friendship between Veena and Shashihaas. They enjoyed each other's company. Veena was impressed with the extensive knowledge that Shashi had. Shashi in turn marveled at the wide spectrum of things that Veena knew and the charming manner in which she would come up with some new aspect adding zest to whatever was being discussed.

Shashi invited her to visit the Indian Embassy in Moscow where he worked as first secretary. The Indian Ambassador Dr. Vyas was a distinguished person who was trusted by the Indian political establishment. He it was that suggested that Veena of Geo—Consult based in London be invited to Moscow since the Indian establishment was interested in oil exploration with a possible tie up with the London firm. When Veena arrived in Moscow there was a brief exchange of views and the Ambassador explained the requirement of the Indian government and elicited Veena's opinion of Geo-Consult's expertise in oil exploration work. Later he entrusted Shashi with the pleasant job of showing her the sights of Moscow.

"I feel nice working with you on helping out Kosmica. I hope that Kosmica soon finds a solution to the cleanser problem" said Veena while she was with Shashi in Moscow

"I'm with you all the way on this. It's most important to stop this unholy cleanser menace somehow without further bloodshed"

Veena spent three days in Moscow. Shashi took her to the famous Kremlin Towers and the Great Kremlin Palace where most Russian czars and rulers had lived. Shashihaas proudly narrated to Veena the history of the Soviet Union officially known as the Union of Soviet Socialist Republics or USSR and how it was unique in so many ways.

"Russia is the world' largest country with a thousand or more major cities spread over a large land mass extending over many time zones and climate zones barring perhaps the tropical zone. Its population is drawn from a variety of ethnicities, religions and languages. While there were many that ruled over it such as the Mongols and others, the Romanov family was the one that consolidated the Russian empire in the 17th century starting with Czar Peter the first. Later it became an important European power after the rule of Queen Catherina the second. "He said

"What about the revolution of 1919 and the world—war victory it achieved over the Nazi juggernaut?" asked Veena.

"Yes, they are crucial events that shaped Russia. America gave it the wherewithal to win the war. Although the ruthless suppression and mass murders during the rule of Stalin and others created a mess Russia quickly recovered and became scientifically and technologically advanced apart from building up its military might as you can now see"

Veena was quite impressed. She noted how she and Shashi though of Indian origin could easily pass off as Russian citizens thanks to their Caucasian features.

With Shashi she also visited the Tretyakov Gallery and the State Historical Museum.

Veena went back to Helsinki and started intensive training for mind-mail empowerment.

It took more than a month for Veena to achieve mind mail savvy. The Kabbalah master told her that surely she must be an incarnation of a great mathematician and that according to him she is destined to sort out a tricky problem affecting the future. Veena was skeptical about this prediction but said nothing.

Veena kept in touch with Heidi her Swedish friend and over a period of a few weeks, was able to gain enough trust for Heidi's boy friend Karl Schumann to ask her along with Heidi to join a party in a posh villa around Hagelund a suburb of Helsingfors.

Veena had told Heidi that she was a spiritualist on a regular schedule of dedicated yoga practice and meditation. Heidi casually informed Karl of it while introducing Veena.

During the party at the villa Karl spoke to Veena while they were somewhat alone.

"Hi, Veena, are you going to the spiritualists conference that I believe is to be held soon?"

"Where?" questioned Veena.

"I'm told it's somewhere in Europe"

"Oh! You mean the really big special one coming up in Spain? It's only for the Grandmasters and I'm not one yet"

"O.K., I understand. Where in Spain but?"

"It's on an Island called Mallorca" said Veena as instructed by Daniel earlier in his dossier.

"Is it sometime this month?"

"I know for sure, it's on the 15th to 20th of next month"

"Thanks. It's not important in any case for me to know"

Karl passed this information on to his handlers at the Cleanser headquarters.

CHAPTER 35

New York

The Arrow projects the picture so that Carlos gets to see the depredation of the cleanser gang and its henchmen.

"It worked"

"It sure did. Now the press is sure that the Hazraras, all four of them, were murdered in the Isle of Wight and is needling the police for answers as to how these bodies were found in the water around their own yacht which earlier the police found did not have the Hazrara family on board"

"How do you think all this will help?"

"Just imagine what the so called spiritual masters must be feeling. They have lost someone who we are told had a secret power to enter a different dimension. It is a big blow to their security system, if they indeed had one. Our mentors have congratulated us and have pumped in a stupendous sum into our coffers. They have also promised to underwrite all losses in our companies due to melt downs in share prices."

"Who found out about Nitin Hazrara's empowerment?"

"There's someone powerful but his identity is a closely guarded secret"

"If that be the case, we and our mentors are unbeatable"

"Touch wood, we'll eliminate all the spiritual fools that talk of reincarnation or after—life"

"Who actually killed the Hazraras?"

"It was a special operation. We knew the route the Hazraras took after they deceived our party at the jetty in the Isle of Wight. We had our expert Nikolai the Russian head of operations to plan the accident at a deserted location. Their car was smashed and it apparently caught fire. We had a long wait before we managed to collect the bodies. We had to hoodwink the locals and collect the bodies saying we are doctors responsible to make post-mortem reports to the police. They believed that we were medical men employed by the government . . . The bodies unfortunately were badly disfigured and their faces unrecognizable"

"You wasted no time and took the bodies stealthily to the Isle and dumped them in the sea where the Yacht was, yes?

"Well something like that I reckon, from what Nikolai told us"

CHAPTER 36

Upper Dimension center

By a unique power of his mentor the Arrow, Carlos is able to visualize certain scenes without being individually empowered to enter those regions.

"Do you know if the empowered person targeted by the evil gang had passed on the key procedure to someone else before the fatality?"

"I've no idea. I do not know of the fatality either. I will come to know pretty soon. However a second empowerment has been in place with a woman. Also there's a congregation of spiritual grandmasters going on in a secret location on planet Earth to take stock of the situation and prepare a roadmap to raise sufficient men and women to fight this new menace on several fronts."

"How invulnerable is this secret location? Because if the spot is revealed there'll be Hades to pay with the cleansers massacring the whole lot of those spiritual grandmasters men and women most mercilessly with no remorse whatsoever"

"It's a top secret location and I believe it's so exclusive it'll be impossible to find out. Also the spiritual grand masters have astral travel advantage"

"Let's hope all goes well"

"There is also some doubt that one of the grand masters is playing a dubious role and is helping the cleansers"

"It seems to be true. It is one of them from the Eastern area I hear. However he is only involved in activity in the fourth and higher dimensions I believe"

The giant duo of guards who looked more like mechanical creatures of metal with mind sense and speech capability resumed their watch around the matrix in the fourth dimension".

CHAPTER 37

Mallorca Island

Carlos observes the great cleanser onslaught guided by the Arrow.

It was a pincer movement. Battle tanks were encircling the area from all sides. There were a great number of armored vehicles with guns mounted on them manned by soldiers in resplendent uniforms. Helicopter gunships and fighter planes were zooming in the skies. Camps with hundreds of tents spread over huge spaces with barbed wire fencing were coming up at a number of places providing accommodation. Special areas were detailed for officers and soldiers with mess facilities and recreation centers. Parade grounds were spruced up. It looked as though a military operation over an extended period was being planned.

"Where's all this leading to?"

"I'm sure it's to get their enemy"

"Who?"

"Whosoever it may be. They sure want to get their enemy so flattened as to leave no trace. The preparation appears to have been planned in great detail and the attack looks imminent any time now. The only point that is delaying the attack seems to be their failure to locate the area where their opposition is centered."

The two hobos got into a pickup truck and started driving out from the area. Romeo Miranda and Francisco Piccolo had come to the place nearly three months back at the instance of their friend and philosopher George Kramer who casually said "listen you guys. If you want to make a quick buck, a few thousand at the least, head straight to the hills around Mallorca off Spain. I hear there's a huge concentration of mercenaries employed by a powerful super rich group of businessmen having billions of dollars to throw around. I'm sure there's going to be a battle of sorts if not a war there"

"Who's on the other side?"

"What does it matter, there's bound to be someone I'm sure."

"How will we get our thousands in such a short period?"

"Money will no doubt pour in along with the huge military force that's around the valley there. There'll be great need for guides and handymen for the force and you fellows are masters in that sort of work aren't you?"

When the duo arrived in Mallorca Island taking their friend Kramer's advice, things started falling into place. They were engaged to work with a team of guides by a local contractor looking every bit a home grown Spaniard addressed as 'Amigo' by all and sundry. Salary offered was way above what they had expected with food and lodging thrown in for free. They were given a pick up truck and were told to keep it. They slogged for three months transporting stuff from one place to another taking turns as driver and handy man. Plenty of booze dirt cheap was there for the asking including tequila Spain's specialty.

"I have a feeling that time's running out and we'll be caught in the crossfire if we stay on here" said Piccolo.

"I bet you're right. We made our dough, now let's scram" said Miranda.

"What are we doing here? I'm with you. We've got our earnings, let's beat it man"

"You said it. Let's lam"

No one stopped them when they left with their truck to get out of the island.

Pretty soon there was a great search on to find and obliterate the spiritual masters and their brood supposed to be in congregation in the Island. The cleanser hordes armed to the teeth were roaming around all over Mallorca.

The spiritual masters were no where to be seen. There was utter consternation. General Mike Smythe who had masterminded the operation was fuming.

"Go find them. Get them out and shoot. No one is to be spared" was his order.

There was tremendous activity to search and destroy the enemy that went on for almost a week

The commanders started asking questions discussing this strange situation.

"There's no one here for us to fight it appears."

"How is it so, after all this preparation spending millions?"

"Well what's a few million dollars to the corporate giants who gave us this job?"

"Heads will roll no doubt."

"I'm not so sure. It keeps happening quite often."

"Let's report back to the General that the whole thing is a red herring"

Surprised though they were, the senior commanders went on staying on the Island along with their huge establishment of men and weapons.

CHAPTER 38

Outer Hebrides

Lewes

Carlos sees and hears the renegade grand master as projected by his mentor the Arrow.

His every move and action was shrouded in utmost secrecy. His identity was unknown and unknowable except for two individuals. The security blanket was total.

The duo of Sir William Witherspoon and Mr. Victor Abrahamson was keenly awaiting his arrival. It was to be their first meeting with the spiritual grandmaster after the fiasco in Mallorca.

"Now, did you tell him about our eagerness to confront and eliminate the spiritual activists?"

"Of course I did, giving no room for any misunderstanding. I didn't however tell him about the blunder in Mallorca and our intelligence failure. We'll tell him now"

"Fine. I have just heard the good news from the council. The empowered person and his family have been eliminated under the very noses of the British police establishment"

"Indeed it is great news. The grandmaster has said that the empowerment however is now with a female person living in England. He has confirmed that he is actively pursuing the elimination of this female"

The grand master had a red carpet reception.

"We were unsuccessful in our attempt to annihilate the spiritualists led by your most hated rival going by the name of 'teacher'. We made preparations to hit their conclave in a Spanish Island location where we were informed they would hold their secret meeting" said Witherspoon.

"You were foolish. Who told you of their secret location?" asked the Grandmaster.

"Our intelligence people from Finland said so. We didn't come to you since we promised that we will consult your holiness only about action in higher dimensions"

"Well let me tell you that I have rendered powerless the empowerment of a female. I now want you to hold your horses and not harm any one till I tell you. The empowerment will be stronger and more powerful if you commit murder and mayhem and I may not be able to help you out then"

"We will tell our people to desist"

"I will prevent precipitate action by any one empowered to access the fourth and higher dimensions"

"We believe your holiness and wish to be guided at every step in this fight. We understand that the spiritualist cadres are in hiding. We will let them stay there for now" said Abrahamson.

CHAPTER 39

Palermo, Sicily

Carlos marvels seeing the important convocation of the spiritual masters thanks to the Arrow's projection.

All those who could make it were there, spiritual grandmasters from all belief systems of the world. As a preliminary requirement names were listed with degrees of achievement in various spiritual domains. In the topmost category designated by the title 'Alfa-yogis' were those having powers of object—creation at will, changing of existing ones, physical disappearance from a spot within seconds apart from the other general capabilities such as astral travel mind mail access and mind reading and visualization. In this Alfa category there were six from India and Nepal, two from China including Tibet, one from Turkey, two from Israel, one from Iran, two from England, two from America, one each from Italy and Portugal, one from Nigeria and lastly one from Egypt. The other grandmasters were categorized as 'beta' and 'theta' yogis according to their capabilities. All three categories came together to form seven groups to represent all capabilities.

There were one hundred forty five spiritual persons both male and female that attended the top secret conclave at Palermo in Sicily. A team of five super masters interacted with each of the groups in turn. There was an 'Open House' session on the closing day.

In this two day conclave many aspects were discussed. Many narrated the manner in which they had countered the assault by the so called Cleanser assassins. It became clear that there was ample success during these encounters for the grandmasters to save themselves. It was achieved without having to harm the opponents permanently or take their life. However the grand masters were sad that they could not save many of their followers in various isolated pockets who had to suddenly face the cleanser menace loosing their lives despite fighting bravely without malice in their hearts against their attackers.

It was revealed that word went round to their followers and associates to lie low for the time being pending collective action by the core group of spiritual leaders.

The major decision taken by the conclave was to invest full authority in the teacher and the core group to find an effective solution to the danger lurking around all spiritualists on earth and implement it without having to call for a conclave again. Daniel on behalf of the teacher assured the conclave that with the cooperation of all of them it shall be done without any loss of time so as to save the situation. He also said that the prime consideration would be to bring about a change of heart in the evil doers and thus eliminate all violent tendencies in them. He further added that he would immediately return back to the teacher and obtain instructions.

CHAPTER 40

London

The Arrow shows Carlos how the spiritual masters came to temporize.

Mason was surprised to see the sudden disappearance of spiritual persons and yoga masters from London and elsewhere in Britain. He wanted to know the reasons for this. He met Bainbridge.

"Have your people decided to give up the fight?"

"No. We have indeed shown our spiritual strength in various ways"

"How"

"When the cleansers came to attack and kill us, we did go through our options"

"Such as what for instance?"

*Some of us took to sudden physical disappearance. Some of us projected phenomenal physical energy to stun the opposition. Others displayed extraordinary martial art skills disorienting the opposition."

"Why then do you feel you are losing out?"

"The cleansers are too many, well organized, well armed and widely positioned all around the world. We in comparison are miniscule, rather isolated and committed to protecting life and abhor violence unafraid of any sacrifice."

"Agreed. May be there are other issues"

"Yes. We are at a great disadvantage because of our basic belief in the sanctity of all forms of life. We are unable to bring ourselves to taking the life of anyone despite being victims of vicious attacks. Because of our spiritual training we nurse no grudge or hatred and have no desire for vengeance which again adds to the problem." Bainbridge was talking to Mason.

"Our boys are confident we will resume the fight soon. They are meanwhile engaged in identifying the Cleanser network and misleading them with bizarre information."

CHAPTER 41

Carlos sees the Cleanser consternation thanks to the Arrow

"Hey, How is it you made such a blunder. Do you know the outfit lost several million dollars, you idiot" shouted General Mike Smythe from Mallorca in Spain on the phone to Schumann in Helsinki after coming to know that he was the informer that caused the fiasco.

Karl Schumann was shocked and scared. "May I know who's on the line please?"

"It's General Smythe, you dunderhead"

"I'm sorry sir, I have no idea what you're saying sir"

'Well, didn't you send the information that the spiritual bigwigs are meeting in Mallorca in Spain?"

"Yes I certainly did Sir and it was a reliable source that I got the information from"

"Who was it?"

"A spiritualist woman called Veena, a friend of Heidi, the girl that I'm engaged to"

"Did you countercheck?"

"No sir. I though that the men in charge at headquarters would have it counterchecked"

"May be you're right. However that woman Veena is apparently a plant by the opposition to hoodwink you and all of us through you. She deserves to die. I'll order her execution but meanwhile if you see her you have to shoot her dead. Is it understood? If I come to know that you have ignored my instruction, you will face severe consequences"

Schumann got really scared. He had not seen the General but was aware that he was a particularly harsh and cruel man that would not stop at anything in his sadistic plans to eliminate the spiritualists. Schuman was an active member of the cleansers club looking after various jobs but was not a part of the murderers' wing of the outfit. He was in a dilemma and decided to avoid Veena at any cost and let the murderers do their job. He met Heidi and warned her not to meet Veena. Heidi was surprised and asked him why. He was evasive and would not reveal anything. Heidi somehow sensed that there was some strong reason which may involve Veena's safety.

General Smythe called up the secret cleanser group based in Helsinki. The group consisted of men and women specially trained for espionage and murder. Two members were detailed with instructions to find and kill Veena.

They were unable to find her in Helsinki and didn't know where she may have gone to. Schumann said that Heidi didn't know either. The search for Veena began in right earnest.

CHAPTER 42

Himalayas

The Arrow shows Carlos how the masters planned a unique experiment.

"We have had to temporize. All are safe for the present. However we are to find a solution before long" said Daniel reporting to the Teacher on returning back to the Himalayas from Palermo.

"It is believed that an Indian astronomer and mathematician Bhascarcharya had found a relationship between the rays of planets and the behavior of humans. He has I believe identified in detail the color of radiation and the planets that have negative rays. His palm leaf manuscripts written in Sanskrit are believed to be lost or misplaced over the past several years. If these could be traced and located perhaps some new way to tackle the problem could emerge. I have an inkling of what the great Bhascara may have suggested and have devised a plan but I feel it is extremely difficult and had never been tried ever. However I cannot proceed till we know Bhascara's identification of the planets giving negative tendencies" the teacher said

"You can't be meaning to tackle the matrix in the fourth dimension you had taught me about"

"You are getting close"

"What is the initial step that we have to take and how do you think the core group could act?"

"You should ask someone in Russia to quickly search their libraries particularly those stocking oriental books and archives for manuscripts in Sanskrit. This language is India specific. We should zero in on Bhascaracharya's"

"If our idea is to find Bhascaracharya's writings, why search in Russia of all places?"

"It is believed that the Nazis had taken two scholars from south India and one from Benares to Germany a few years before the Second World War along with many original manuscripts dealing with physical sciences, astronomy and mathematics written in Sanskrit and Pali languages. It is said that these manuscripts were translated into German. It is also said that Russian secret agents later managed to take away the original manuscripts from Germany to Russia to benefit their research programs. It is generally known that these manuscripts have been placed in the archives of libraries there.

Luckily for us, a team of two spiritually empowered persons is now working browsing the matrix of the humans and the limbed beings that is in the fourth dimension to identify the phenomenon of those with their glow factor predominantly of a distinct color or a combination of colors. They have concluded that the cleansers and particularly their leaders would have perhaps the highest negative glow and absence of tinges of positive colors"

"Who is the one leading the browsing team?"

"The leader is Brahmapragjna that had initiated you. He has the ultimate responsibility of dealing with criminal minds once their identity is well established. He is presently in the process of forming his team that he feels will represent the spiritual beliefs of all humans coming from every religious background, be it Christian, Jewish, Hindu, Islamic, Buddhist, Zoroastrian or other and relate the content to the control matrix modus operandi especially with the glow factor content of each individual now living. The secret is to combine the latest scientific achievements using satellite technology that is recently proven and the concentrated power of spiritualism"

"With your vision there is no doubt whatsoever that the project will be a success"

"Thank you. It is now most essential for us to find the lost manuscripts of Bhascara more than anything else to proceed with the solution without fear of failure. I bank on you to play a crucial role" said the teacher.

CHAPTER 43

Helsinki

Carlos guided by his mentor gets a glimpse of Veena's activity.

Veena started communicating with Daniel by mind mail.

She received an urgent request to seek in Russia certain manuscripts written in Sanskrit by Bhascaracharya the Indian scientist, astronomer and mathematician who hailed from an area she knew very well.

She was thrilled since the legend of Bhascara and his daughter Lilavati fascinated her from childhood. She had known some of the mathematical riddles Bhascara had set for his daughter in lilting Sanskrit poetry. One such described a lotus flower with its stem in a lake and an observer standing on the bank while the flower's stem is bent by a slow wafting wind to make it touch the water's surface. The riddle was to calculate the distance of the observer from the flower which involved the application of the theorem of Pythagoras and Apastambha.

Some words of this beautiful poetic riddle in Sanskrit such as "Mandam mandam chalitamanile quapi drushtve thataake" stayed on in her mind from her childhood days giving her great joy.

The first thing Veena did was to look up the entry in the encyclopedia about Bhascara. The following was what she found.

"Bháscara Áchárya (1114-1185) India

Bhascara (sometimes called Bhascaracharya) who lived in the 12th century was perhaps the greatest of the Hindu mathematicians. He made significant achievements in several fields of mathematics including some

161

Europe wouldn't learn until the time of Euler. His textbooks dealt with many matters, including solid geometry, combinations, and advanced arithmetic methods. He was also an astronomer. (It is sometimes claimed that his equations for planetary motions anticipated the Laws of Motion discovered by Kepler and Newton, but this claim is doubtful.) In algebra, he solved various equations including 2nd-order Diophantine, quartic, Brouncker's and Pell's equations. His "Chakravala method," an early application of mathematical induction to solve 2nd-order equations, has been called "the finest thing achieved in the theory of numbers before Lagrange." (Earlier Hindus, including Brahmagupta, contributed to this method.) In several ways he anticipated calculus: he used Rolle's Theorem; he may have been first to use the fact that $d\sin x = \cos x \cdot dx$; and he once wrote that multiplication by $0/0$ could be "useful in astronomy." In trigonometry, which he valued for its own beauty as well as practical applications, he developed spherical trig and was first to present the identity

$$\sin a+b = \sin a \cdot \cos b + \sin b \cdot \cos a$$"

Veena felt a bond with this great astronomer scientist cum mathematician who was also a poet and an aesthetic person.

Bhascara's achievements came centuries before similar discoveries in Europe. It is an open mystery whether any of Bhascara's teachings trickled into Europe in time to influence its Scientific Renaissance.

Veena was happy and proud that she was born in Bhascara's land. She had enjoyed reciting his poetry to impress her peers while in school.

Veena set about to hunt for the manuscripts right away. Shasihaas helped her with a detailed list of Oriental libraries and archives where such manuscripts could be found. There were five of them located one each in Moscow, Nizhniy Novgorod, Yekaterinburg, Minsk and St. Petersburg.

Veena over a period of two weeks went to all the above libraries and pored through the lists of documents lying in each of these places. She found many Sanskrit texts of Vedic origin including the Upanishads and also other works of Hindu scholars and Buddhist preachers. There were manuscripts in Paali and some other ancient languages of Indo-German vintage. She however did not find any works of Bhascara. She reported back to Daniel utterly disappointed. Daniel said that she should stay on in Moscow and continue the search and not return to Helsinki till he told her to. He asked Shashihaas to look after Veena and assist her.

"Our people have tried but have not found any of Bhascara's writings" said Daniel to the Teacher.

"We have to keep trying. I have asked two scholars from India to try and get them. They obtained a lot of manuscripts of Bhascara but none of them dealing with astronomy or planetary radiation"

"I'll ask Veena and Shasihaas to keep looking in the smaller cities" said Daniel taking leave of the Teacher.

Veena stayed on in Russia and continued her search for the manuscripts.

She and Shashi planned to go along looking for the manuscripts in the smaller libraries and archives in various locations in Russia as suggested by Daniel. Veena said "Let me start with the European part of Russia where the chances of finding such manuscripts are more"

"Yes I agree with you. Incidentally I have just now received information that some people are looking for you in Russia. This is a serious situation. I have a feeling it's the cleanser goons who may have come from Helsinki. I've managed to get permission from the Ambassador to accompany you and be your protector"

"What luck? Be my guest. I've a job to do and I'll do it cleansers or no cleansers."

On that note Veena and Shashi started their mission. One of the places on their list was Kirov on the river Vyatka. The archives—library was close to the popular Assumption Cathedral a tourist attraction. They found the place which was quite huge.

"We're tourists from London and are looking for some 12th century manuscripts written in Sanskrit" Veena told the main librarian of the place.

"We have a huge collection. Please accompany my assistant to the basement section" he said detailing a person to take them down.

In Kirov, Veena and Shashi had a first hand experience of the cleanser gang's ruthlessness. Apparently the chief librarian was an accomplice. Their escort while leading them down to the basement section asked them to wait at the landing corridor for a minute. Shashi immediately sensed that something was amiss. Sure enough he could spot a man at the side of the stair case making some sort of a sign to some one else who perhaps was ready on the lower steps. Shashi lost no time. He grabbed Veena's hand and started running up the stairs to the ground level. There were shots heard and the sound of footsteps of those chasing them. Luckily they escaped just in time and went straight back to their hotel.

Veena more or less exhausted all avenues to find the manuscripts but was unsuccessful and in desperation asked Daniel the exact subject of Bhascaracharya's manuscripts she was supposedly looking for.

"It had to do with radiation of planets that negatively affected human behavior and the color that signaled the absorption of such radiation" He said.

Veena set to thinking and reminiscing. She slept over it for a week. Suddenly one morning she thought of the well—filled book of quotations she maintained with fresh entries as and when they took her fancy. The book was lying in London.

She spoke with Bose 'Hi, this is Veena. I need a favor. Could you please get across to my digs in London and get my book of quotations lying in my display cupboard and post it to me? It's rather urgent"

"No hassle. You'll receive the book promptly. Cheerio for now" Bose promised.

The book arrived soon enough. Veena remembered a quotation of a scholar Vidyadhara known to be a student of Bhascara about color and human nature and planets. She wasn't sure of the content as she never considered it important or path breaking. She now searched for and found it. It ran as below;

> Satah purushaat Janma Graha
> Viseshena varnam samupastitam
> Neela Varna raahityam
> Duswabhavadhikya hethuhu.
>   Tatvyathirekam suswabhavapoornathvam.
> Iti dwau samana grahaanaam
> Tadupagraha Kiranena sambhavanti.
> (Mama Guru Bhascaracharya prakatitam)

{In a living human, the planetary aspect at the time of birth results in color. The absence of blue color indicates bad nature. The opposite indicates fullness of good nature. This effect is due to the shining rays of two similar planets and their sub planets.—(This is declared by my guru Bhascaracharya.)}

Veena transmitted this information to Daniel without delay. Daniel in turn relayed it to the teacher.

"Wonderful. We have the answer. The two similar planets are Uranus and Neptune. Triton is Neptune's moon. I already have the calculations ready. We have to get the space scientists to do the needful which I shall explain in detail. Brahmapragjna will now proceed with identifying the deficiency of color blue in the matrix units of the fourth dimension. Thank you indeed. You should thank the girl. Her name is Veena is isn't it? She in any case has to help out with the project as she is already empowered to access the fourth dimension" said the teacher

CHAPTER 44

Helsinki

The Arrow now shows the supra human travel details as in a movie, to Carlos.

"You have to urgently travel to the fourth dimension" said Daniel

"Just let me know the procedure so that I could go" replied Veena.

"You are the empowered one as I had informed earlier. You close your eyes in deep meditation while in the lotus pose and chant the word 'Soham' for 108 times and all will be revealed for your astral travel. Best of luck"

Veena did as advised. At the end of her chanting, there was a sudden transformation in her environment. Everything went dark while a pathway of light was visible.

"Start moving forward in the path of light" said a voice heard by Veena. Pretty soon she felt her body move at unimaginable speed while her mind remained joyous happy and utterly peaceful.

"Veena come to join me here" was what she heard and saw a speck of crimson light. She found her body wasn't visible anymore and she was herself a speck of light.

Exchange of words happened in a strange manner. It seemed as though the mind mechanism had gone to higher levels of interaction. The body aspect seemed irrelevant.

Brahmapragjna it was that interacted with Veena. They discussed the planetary radiation effect. Veena realized that she was none other than Bhascaracharya reborn as Veena. She immediately accessed the memory bank that came rushing over to her with all the knowledge of

Bhascara. Brahmapragjna had known that he was a reincarnation of Rene Descartes who lived from the fag end of the 16th century till the middle of the 17th century. He now understood the concept of color blue in the units of the matrix. Veena in her new capacity helped out Brahmapragjna to coordinate the solution to the problem of eliminating the impact of negative rays of Uranus and Neptune and of its moon Triton on the units of the matrix in the fourth dimension.

Daniel was informed of this unique solution. Brahmapragjna introduced Veena to others working with him in the team.

Veena returned to her original three dimensional spaces on earth.

CHAPTER 45

Moscow

Carlos guided by the Arrow witnesses the coming together of science, technology and spiritualism.

"Are you sure it can be done?" asked the first one.

"Of course without doubt" answered the second.

"It'll then be a strange unheard of collaboration of the power of applied science and the power of spirituality" commented the third.

"Indeed. It'll help save the highest human values and bring peace to the world without shedding blood" said the fourth.

This exchange went on at an exclusive secret meeting held by the world's top scientists and researchers with the spiritual masters. The teacher had assiduously prepared the ground for this important interaction by visiting the presidents and prime ministers of the most technologically relevant countries as also the German chancellor and explained to them the enormous importance of the intended project. The heads of governments after being convinced of its viability agreed to send their experts including the head honchos of their nuclear and space research organizations. This was how the conclave came about with the scientists and technologists from countries across the world interacting with six spiritual grandmasters of different religious backgrounds with Daniel heading the team of grandmasters. Daniel asked Parama to give a presentation on the basis of the teacher's project with the recent fourth dimension inputs from Brahmapragjna and Veena for changing the behavior pattern of living humans using the ' Radiation color-glow theory' called the 'Blue truth'.

Parama made his presentation by giving an exhaustive account of the concept of a set of unalterable laws concerning the cycles of birth, existence and reincarnation of all things without exception from the smallest sub-atomic particle to the biggest planets and stars and the control matrices for the limbed creatures including humans located in higher dimensions and those located on Earth for other categories including insects bacteria and particles of matter existing in our Sun-centered planetary system. He described the color code and the planetary radiation effects which formed a part of the discovery recorded by the Indian mathematician and astronomer Bhascaracharya in the 12th century. He then answered various questions during the presentation.

He then came to the specific subject under discussion and went on to say "Our planetary system is a maze, the terrestrials Mercury, Venus, Earth and Mars and the gas giants Saturn, Uranus, Neptune and Pluto orbiting our Sun since the beginning of time that no one can discern with any degree of astronomical exactitude"

"It is beyond doubt that these planets have a direct influence on the pattern of events that happen in the context of limbed living beings on earth at any given point in time including the individual's behavior pattern" said Parama and continued

'We researched the Eastern astrology concepts of the so called 'kundalis' or horoscopes of individual humans represented by twelve spaces called houses inside a four sided figure. These spaces were obtained by drawing the figure of a square or rectangle on paper with its opposite end—points connected internally by two straight lines and its mid points connected inwards again to form an enclosed square or rectangle giving rise to twelve spaces in the diagram. These spaces are called houses and are numbered in a particular way. Each house is influenced by the transit of planets of our solar system defining the positive and negative attributes of each entity in the time frames between its birth or incarnation and death or de-incarnation. We came up on the factor of color and after a great amount of research and thought hit upon the idea of negative radiation affecting the behavior pattern of individuals.

An important aspect is the location in the fourth dimension of the control matrix relating to humans and other limbed units. The planetary radiation is acute and complex in this dimension and not simple as in the third dimension

"Uranus that has a 3% larger radius and a 15% smaller mass compared to Neptune and has an orbital time of 84 years while the orbital time of Neptune is almost twice at 165 years. Their rotation period is almost the same at 17 hrs and 16 hrs. Our research has also considered Triton the largest moon of Neptune which has retrograde motion around the planet. The combined movement and radiation of these three showed up a possible 80 year cycle of blacking out the color 'blue positive' of the glow factor superimposed on the symbols of living beings in the control matrix that is located in the fourth dimension. This effect could result in infusing negative and evil tendencies causing violence and hatred. The highly blue tinged symbols escape this influence but those with minimal blue are greatly affected making the individuals into criminals characterized by violent negative behavior and uncalled for hatred against all those coming in the way of their exploitation.

We have pinpointed with great accuracy the time and duration when the direct influence of radiation will affect the relevant matrix. The influence once received by the individual symbols will last for approximately one cycle of orbiting time of Uranus. Once we succeed in blocking this radiation its influence is obliterated and the glow factor stays untouched. Negativity will then have no place in the behavior pattern of those humans on earth that now have decreased blue tinge in their glow factor. By barring this radiation the blue color is restored for them. This effect will last for an 80 year cyclic time frame" said Parama concluding

"What is the overall concept for our combined project?" asked Dr. Bromfield `the expert from the U.S. Space administration.

"We are eager to formulate the requirements for organizing logistic and financial support as may be needed for the project from the government and from private funding" said Kruspoyev of the Soviet Union.

"We pinpoint the orbits based on our research for three satellites that will have to be launched. The time of launch will more or less coincide with the calculations of the twin retrograde movements of Uranus and Neptune the planets with almost identical inner characteristics and also Triton the huge moon of Neptune"

'You are to launch the three satellites from pre-determined locations in Europe, Russia and the United States for simultaneous coverage of the entire matrix spectrum through the chosen orbits. The exact time and date will be calculated by our team of spiritualists while the locations will be fixed by your team on the basis of launch convenience for attaining the predetermined orbits"

"What about building the satellites?" interposed another space scientist.

"The designs have been finalized by the committee of the International space research council and approved by its technical wing. As of now we have the infrastructure and the manufacturing units in place in the three countries mentioned namely the USSR, USA and Italy." said the British representative Dr. William Gillespie of the ISRC.

Detailed discussions followed for the next two days working round the clock. Communications and instructions were flying around the world from the space scientists and satellite technologists and scientists. Preparations were initiated promptly at all the three chosen sites within a few days after the meeting concluded. Immediate assembling of satellites with their sensitive equipment with special variations in each case was taken up on a priority basis. The financial aspect was being organized from Falmouth in Cornwall and other places around the world.

The teacher spoke to Daniel and advised him on certain matters that are to be kept in mind.

Daniel had a one to one meeting with each of the top men Dr. Bromfield, Kuuspoyev and Dr. Gillespie and conveyed the thinking of his teacher. He then met them together with Parama forming a well knit team for operational control. An exclusive communication and interaction policy was agreed upon. Certain other security concerns were discussed in general. It was decided that Daniel would interact with Kruspoyev on a regular basis.

CHAPTER 46

The arrow gives his narration and guides Carlos through the cleanser network's spying and destructive moves and the ultimate result.

The proverbial saying 'there's many a slip between the cup and the lip' proved itself in no uncertain a manner. The cleanser outfit looking for Veena reported back to its headquarters of their failure in Kirov and suggested that she may have been saved by Shashihaas of the Indian embassy in Russia which must have been because of some information leak that alerted him.

Immediately Shashihaas was targeted by the cleanser group and all his activities and correspondence was monitored regularly. Additionally there was some information that some experiments by way of satellite launch technology were being planned by a powerful international organization. This was conveyed confidentially to the big bosses. Sir William Witherspoon discussed the matter with Victor Abrahamson.

"There's nothing to worry. The so called powerful international organization is the ISRC International Space Research Council, funded by many countries. I've made fool—proof arrangements to spy on the scientists and engineers associated with this outfit which is in the business of developing the latest technology for satellite launching. I have information that some experiments are going on at various sites in this regard" said Victor.

"Are they trying to launch some spy satellites?"

"I'm not sure"

"We cannot afford to be complacent in these matters. You better order our men to destroy the experimental sites and equipment if it is detrimental to our cause. No cost is too high for achieving this objective."

"I'll throw the treasury open if need be to ensure our success "said Abrahamson

"Go ahead" said Witherspoon.

Abrahamson got in touch with the operational command heads of the cleanser groups in Moscow, Atlanta and Istanbul and passed on fresh instructions. A core group was formed at the main centre headed by Dr. Shaw with six others as members. A security and intelligence gathering tactician Dr. Edmond Shingle with his wide-spread team was recruited to develop a spy network in the ISRC. Shingles proceeded with speed and purpose and started a regular reporting system of information to the Cleanser core group and a follow up cell for acting on suggestions made by the group. He personally briefed Dr. Shaw from time to time.

The core group came to know of the experimental satellites to be launched from three locations presumed to be for experimental data gathering and similar other purposes. 'This vital information was revealed by none other than the man controlling the space project of the ISRC and hence beyond any doubt' said Dr.Shingle in his top secret personal briefing report to Dr. Shaw. There was an apparent lull in processing of information received from the spy team for a while following this authentic information from the horse's mouth as it were.

Things however turned ugly and upside down when an input came from an operative from Russia that the satellites were indeed being launched for an ulterior purpose guided by a spiritual master known as Daniel.

"I want the minutest details of every satellite and every launch pad handling it" said Dr. Shaw to Dr. Shingle adding "I do not care how you get it but get it for God's sake whatever the cost" A massive pro-active phase was put in place and constant monitoring and analysis commenced in right earnest by the cleanser core group and associates.

Meanwhile work progressed at a fast pace by the ISRC group with full cooperation and backing of the governments of various countries. Launch sites were selected and satellites were being assembled and made ready. Launching rockets were positioned at the sites and all systems and control mechanisms checked and verified.

It took over three months to prepare the launch program at the selected sites.

The activists of the cleanser outfit were getting ready to spoil the show. The three locations they had identified at Izmir in Turkey, Gdansk in Poland and Tacoma in the USA were on the radar of the outfit and preparations were underway to blast the sites out of existence together with their rockets and satellites.

After a period of nearly four months, the special satellites were ready for launching on a Wednesday at different times from their locations as per the advice of Daniel's team of spiritual masters who were constantly in touch with the space scientists and engineers.

The launch was formally announced by the ISRC for take off on the second Wednesday of July and one could see a flurry of activity. The cleanser team was ready with plans to aerially bomb the sites at midnight on Tuesday to eliminate the risk of any last-minute failure.

The cleansers carried out their nefarious action on Tuesday night by carpet bombing the sites destroying the launch rockets and their payloads completely, turning the sites into chaotic masses of debris.

Wednesday came.

"Unexpected and complete success" shouted Dr. Shaw adding "The sites were bombed out with great precision and the rockets completely destroyed with their payloads."

"Congrats. Great work. Thank all the team members and declare a phenomenal bonus" said Abrahamson and immediately conveyed the news to Witherspoon. Celebrations broke out in all Cleanser strongholds.

However the story didn't end there. The story was different in many ways as far as Daniel and Kruspoyev were concerned. Meticulous planning to misguide the cleanser spy network was carefully put in place. Pseudo activity with dummy rockets and make-believe satellites went on at a furious pace at the false sites of Izmir, Gdansk and Tacoma. Meanwhile all arrangements with great care were made at the secret locations of Nicosia in Cyprus, Rostock in Poland and Vancouver in Canada placing the correct satellite-payloads and rockets there. On Wednesday these powerful rockets were launched and the satellites were correctly placed in their orbits in space at pre-decided times.

The machinations of the Cleansers came to naught since the game was played in a masterly manner misguiding the Cleanser spy network by conducting a mock exercise at each of the dummy locations which were indeed bombed out by the cleansers with glee and pride spending millions of dollars.

It took considerable ingenuity and precision on the part of the ISRC to organize the genuine launches from secret and undisclosed locations thus hoodwinking the cleansers designs.

The three satellites were placed in orbits exactly as planned. The spiritual masters held a mind mail cum visualization conclave and directed their combined cosmic power to assist the blockage of negative radiation on the matrix in the fourth dimension thus leaving the blue tinge of the glow factors of a majority of units of the matrix untouched and in fact boosting the blue tinge where it was low in several thousand units.

CHAPTER 47

Yarmouth

The Arrow shows Carlos, how Nitin and family get saved.

It was nothing short of a miracle that saved Nitin Hazrara, Tavleen, Shreya and Shankar at the nick of time from an unimaginably horrible death. They in fact saw their station wagon smashed to bits minutes after they were out of it, a big truck impacting it at speed. The area was an isolated stretch with apparently no one around.

"How do you like it?" asked the grandmaster who with his assistant had saved them.

"We are speechless with wonder and gratitude" said Tavleen.

Hazrara and the kids echoed the sentiment.

"This may be good in a way. It gives you freedom to act incognito if the opposition takes you for dead. Let us burn up the wagon"

"Yes indeed. We will follow your every word and instruction"

The heavy truck they found was empty of its driver who may have jumped out and fled just before the impact which was no doubt pre-planned and deliberate. Pretty soon their wagon was put to fire by the young master Alberto Rimini.

"The fun starts now" said the young man. "We will take you to Yarmouth forthwith"

"Don't we have to obtain some transport to do that?" questioned Shreya.

'We always carry our transport facility with us don't we?" asked the elder grand master.

"Yes indeed, we do" said Rimini.

The Hazrara family was curious and confused.

In the next minute a fantastic and miraculous thing happened.

Hazrara and the family disappeared and reappeared in a jiffy at the private jetty at Yarmouth. The Hazraras now believed that the impossible is only for the likes of them and not for the spiritual masters. They were thankful that the powers that be are with them.

They made it to Falmouth in Cornwall away from London in the speed launch waiting for them at the jetty.

Nitin made a vital decision. The family will lie low but actively help out their saviors in whichever way they need. As a first step they bought an isolated but decent cottage in Falmouth in Alberto Rimini's name. The latest communication equipment was installed there. A few million pounds sterling lying in Grindlays Bank, London in Tavleen's name was accessed and transferred to a trust account for which Tavleen was the sole authorized signatory.

Nitin however was active in lending support to Kosmica in all possible ways including remittance of funds. He established contact with Margie Boyd and obtained her assurance that strict secrecy will be maintained and the fact of his being alive will not be revealed under any circumstances. He convinced Margie that he was not fully fit and that his instructions should be carried out as though they are from her. He made sure that his phone calls are never traced to reveal the location. He told Rimini that he would pump in all the money the family controlled for any scheme that the spiritual masters wanted implemented.

CHAPTER 48

London

Carlos thanks to the Arrow gets to know more about the cleanser killers.

"The job is done. I smashed their wagon to bits. All of them are dead" said the driver of the truck from a telephone booth a mile or so away from the action site on the approach road to Yarmouth.

"You may now arrange to collect the bodies" he added.

The truck driver had jumped out before the impact, saw the colossal damage and had quickly run to the booth.

"Thanks and congrats, we are sending Mike Trench who has been waiting nearby with his crew. You wait at the booth and take him to the site when he gets there. He will deal with the bodies"

Trench arrived soon after in an ambulance with his crew. He picked the driver up and reached the action scene. He was dismayed at the sight.

"The station Wagon is burnt to ashes and the bodies as well" Said Mike to the handler in charge of this operation. There was consternation and disbelief at the handler's end. However the handler quickly thought out a plan to protect him and his cronies. He gave instructions.

"We have to urgently find other bodies to replace these. Get in touch with hospitals in London and elsewhere in Europe and get the corpses of a man of around 52 years, a woman around forty five years, a 16 year old boy and a fourteen year old girl all of them south Asian, Greek or Turkish looking. You have an unlimited budget to get them. The bodies are to be shot and mutilated carefully to prevent identification except for their ethnic origin. Get on with the job. We have very little time" said the handler.

Mike Trench set his team to accomplish the difficult task. Several phone calls were made to the agents that deal with the procurement and sale of bodies to medical colleges and research outfits buying them out from hospitals. Agents in England, Greece and Turkey were targeted. It took three days to get hold of four corpses of the specified age groups from hospital morgues in Athens, Greece. They were after due preparation as instructed by the handler transported secretly to the Isle of Wight and dumped in the sea around the yacht Solaris. Trench's handler Malankayev kept the whole matter a secret and informed his co-conspirators that the bodies of the Hazraras were recovered from the smashed van and were prepared as required to show gunshot wounds and dumped next to their yacht in the Isle of White. He never told them that the bodies were unrecognizably mutilated before being thrown in the sea.

CHAPTER 49

Yarmouth

Carlos is made aware by the Arrow, of activity in the higher dimensions.

"It's time now for you to access the fourth dimension" said Parama, the grand master speaking to Nitin.

"Is there a specific task for me, noble sir?"

"Yes there is. You will meet up with Brahmapragjna and Veena who are out there finalizing a solution for the cleanser problem"

"How will I get to meet them?"

"Things will happen in a particular sequence and Brahmapragjna will guide you from the very beginning like he did for Veena"

"May I know a little bit more about them please?"

Parama put Nitin wise to the background of the duo and also explained the work they were engaged in. "Once you understand the nature of the solution, it will be your job to tie up whatever finances that may be needed and negotiate with the governments concerned"

"It suits me fine"

Nitin accessed the fourth dimension under the continual guidance of Brahmapragjna and met up with him and also with Veena.

On gaining access to the new dimension Nitin became super conscious and could see his own past. He realized that he was none other than Aaron Livni a prosperous Jewish American financial wizard in his previous incarnation. It came to him as a surprise.

CHAPTER 50

London

Carlos guided by the Arrow watches the grand finale.

They were all there. The Hazrara family, the grand masters, the scientists, Veena and the three Prgjnas, Surprisingly enough there were also the armament bigwigs Witherspoon, Abrahamson and others including diplomats.

It was a grand celebration with the media in full attendance.

The surprise item was the presence of the Hazrara family before the media.

Parama rose and addressed the congregation.

"An apology is due. We invited all of you, your Excellencies, ladies and gentlemen to kindly attend this get together without mentioning the occasion. I would now seek your kind permission to rectify this omission. We have several exciting things to reveal. Firstly I shall with great pleasure present before you in flesh and blood the Hazrara family who had been presumed to have been brutally murdered and thrown into the sea around their own yacht.

Secondly Mr. Hazrara will narrate the travails he and his family went through and how they lived to tell us the tale."

"After Mr. Hazrara's narration you will see in person the so called 'renegade great grand master' who will tell us how he made it possible to stall the Cleanser program to a large extent by holding them back till the ultimate solution was achieved.

He it was who saved the spiritualists from grave danger by apparently hitching up with the opposition. Today both the former cleansers and the people appreciate his grand and timely action. We also have here the top tycoons who started the cleanser movement due to a misunderstanding of the nature of the spiritualists' view of humanity. They are now fully with us and according to the code of repentance all is forgiven and they now will play a huge part in alleviation of suffering of the poor and dispossessed of our world. Their billions will now be spent to achieve a hunger-less humanity assured of shelter and protection.

With the past put in perspective and hailing the present harmony and worldwide peace and rejection of violence, all of us including the ex-opposition are extremely happy and joyous. Now dealing with things beyond our common ken, the sage Brahmapragjna will give an overview of the blocking of the negative planetary radiation and its effect of erasing the criminal aspect from the Cleansers' minds."

Parama invited the others to speak.

All of them spoke as expected and the celebration was a great success. The one major point that stood out was the frank speech by Chandrapragjna of Chinese ancestry. He said "I was the renegade grand master. I was told to take up that role by my Guru Brahmapragjna. He convinced me of the importance of such a role. He rightly pointed out the relevance of the ancient dictum "Nonviolence is the supreme righteousness' and showed me the path of evolution to a future of a world without wars and violence on this planet Earth which is our abode" and added.

"Today I join the rest of the world in thanking my Guru from the bottom of my heart"

EPILOGUE

There was a stupendous transformation in attitudes. Armament magnates Witherspoon, Abrahamson and others turned a new leaf and started cutting down drastically on production targets worldwide. The cleanser groups and activists were being disbanded and the international council headed by Oscar Miller was dissolved and their murdering squads in various countries in Europe and elsewhere were told to call it a day. The word went round that the spiritualists are not to be harassed anymore and that a free hand be given to them to preach, train and practice. The Governments of various countries came forward to reimburse the cost of the launch of satellites and the cost of their upkeep and of monitoring stations. Seminars were organized in many countries on the importance of spiritual practices by masters and grand masters of all religious backgrounds. A general atmosphere of bonhomie descended in the religious centers of all major religions and the specter of inter religious bickering and intolerance ended. A significant change in orthodox quarters sparked many open house sessions to understand the precepts of the sacred books and scriptures of different religions. Thus the purpose of the satellite launch was achieved and criminal mindsets cleansed themselves.

Alberto Rimini the person that was later to interact with Carlos in Bandhavadurg was granted access to the matrices on Earth pending further spiritual progress to gain entry to higher dimensions and matrices. Rimini went to India and became a spiritual master. Veena and Shasihaas were united in wedlock with the blessings of the teacher and Daniel.

Chandrapragjna who was the so called 'renegade spiritual grandmaster' went back to run the Ashram in Katmandu while Brahmapragjna immersed himself in research with Daniel and Alberto assisting him. They took up residence in a hill station in western India.